Other books by the Author:

Troy

Luna

Leslie

Perseus

Richard Matturro

Drawings by

Mary Trevor Thomas

Livingston Press

The University of West Alabama

Copyright © 2010 Richard Matturro
Copyright artwork © 2010 Mary Trevor Thomas
All rights reserved, including electronic text
isbn 13 978-1-60489-053-2 trade paper
isbn 13 978-1-60489-052-5, lib. bind.
Library of Congress Control Number 2010920379
Printed on acid-free paper.
Printed in the United States of America,
Publishers Graphics
Hardcover binding by: Heckman Bindery

Typesetting and page layout: Joe Taylor
Proofreading: Tricia Taylor,
Rufus Alsabrook

Cover design: Mary Trevor Thomas
Cover layout: Mary Trevor Thomas

This is a work of fiction.
Surely you know the rest: any resemblance
to persons living or dead is coincidental.

Livingston Press is part of The University of West Alabama,
and thereby has non-profit status.
Donations are tax-deductible:
brothers and sisters, we need 'em.

first edition
6 5 4 3 3 2 1

Perseus

For Carol

Contents

I.	Shower of Gold	1
II.	Messenger	10
III.	Gifts of the Gods	20
IV.	Directives	27
V.	Damsel	33
VI.	Joppa	40
VII.	Sea Serpent	47
VIII.	Bedfellows	52
IX.	Thief	59
X.	Cimmeria	65
XI.	Gray Women	70
XII.	Divestment	76
XIII.	Owl	81
XIV.	Rites of Bacchus	88
XV.	Apparitions	94
XVI.	Land of the Hyperboreans	100
XVII.	Muse's Dream	107
XVIII.	Circle	115
XIX.	Medusa	120
XX.	Seriphos	126
XXI.	Blood Ties	131
XXII.	Orphans	139
XXIII.	Argos	144
XXIV.	Beachcombers	152

ναυσὶ δ οὔτε μεξὸς ἰών κεν εὔροις
ἐσ Ὑπερβορέων ἀγῶνα θαυματὰν ὁδόν.

Pindar *Pythian* X 29-30

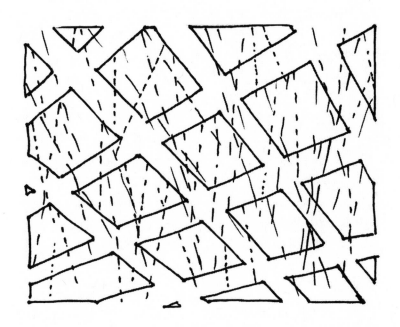

I
Shower of Gold

"A Gorgon's head?!"

"Medusa's head, to be specific," the blond young man corrected her. "It was the first thing I could think of."

"Oh my God," Danae sighed. She sat down at the rustic wooden table, one of the few pieces of furniture in the spare, two-room dwelling they shared. The thick black hair that fell on her shoulders framed an aristocratic face, not always so well acquainted with poverty. She leaned her cheek on her hand. "I have only one son, and he has to be an idiot."

"Well, I meant it as a joke, for God's sake," Perseus explained. "He wanted a horse. That's why he summoned everyone to the palace in the first place. It's some sort of a tax so he can send a herd to King Pelops of Mycenae as a gift. A diplomatic gesture, I gather, from one Greek king to another. But how the hell could I come up with a horse? We can hardly even afford a goat. So I told him he might as well ask me to bring him Medusa's head."

"And he did," Danae concluded dryly.

Perseus slumped his lanky frame into a chair across from his mother. "You don't think he could be serious, do you? I mean, there is no Medusa. There are no Gorgons. It's just a fairy tale."

Danae shook her head. "An idiot. Zeus had nothing better to do than to give me an idiot."

"Well, Mother, honestly! Polydectes couldn't really believe in Gorgons, could he? He's not that dumb."

She leveled her gaze at him. "Perseus, son of my loins—"

"I wish you wouldn't always say that," he murmured, shifting uneasily in his seat.

"Son of my loins," she repeated more insistently, "don't you understand? It doesn't matter if there are Gorgons or not, or if King Polydectes believes in them. You fell right into his hands, and now he can use you to get what he wants."

"What does he want?"

"Me."

"*You?*"

"Close your mouth. You look like an imbecile."

"Well, I don't understand. What would he want you for?"

Danae put her hands on her hips and looked at him expectantly.

"Noooo." Perseus drew out the word, shaking his head. "That's not it. That couldn't be it."

"Oh? Why couldn't it?"

"Well, you're ..."

"Yes?"

He shrugged his shoulders. "Well, aren't you too old for ...?"

She arched an eyebrow. "I'm thirty-eight, and despite the fact that I have a dimwit for a son, I still happen to be a beautiful woman."

"Well, of course you're beautiful to me."

"You can just wipe that condescending smile off your moronic face and keep your lame compliments to yourself. You wouldn't know a beautiful woman if she leapt up and bit you in the ass. At any rate, Polydectes has sent messages to me. It's clear what he wants."

"But I still don't understand. What does that have to do with the Gorgon's head?"

His mother sighed. "Son of my loins, before today everybody, Polydectes included, thought of you as an impediment to anyone's improper designs on me. Next to a husband, which I don't have, a grown son is supposed to be the best protection a lone woman has in the world. Heaven knows, in a real pinch you'd be about as useful to me as a second—"

Perseus coughed and looked away.

"Well, anyway," she continued, "nobody but me knew how useless you were. Now, thanks to your ridiculous statement—which everyone heard—you've made it easy for the good king."

"How?"

"If you don't bring him the Gorgon's head, he can have you executed. To save your neck, I'll have to give in to him."

Perseus stared at her, the import of her words sinking in.

"Understand now?"

He lowered his eyes, his voice barely audible. "I'm sorry."

"Oh, hell, it's all right. Worse things have happened to people. I suppose I can get used to Polydectes. He is an ugly son of a bitch though, with a pot belly to boot."

"*Shit!* " Perseus exclaimed, banging his fist on the table. "*Shit, shit, shit!* "

His mother rolled her eyes heavenward. "Are you listening, Zeus? That's your son being articulate again."

Perseus scowled. "Do you have to keep up that silly fiction—even now?"

"What silly fiction?"

"That Zeus is my father. Zeus isn't my father. I doubt there even is a Zeus."

"There's a Zeus," Danae assured him, nodding knowingly.

"I don't think so."

"We've become an atheist now, have we?"

"I'm not an atheist. I'm an agnostic."

"Pardon me."

"But I'll tell you one thing," he added, "I don't believe in Zeus or in any of that whole criminal pantheon."

Danae glanced at the ceiling again. "Forgive him, Zeus. He knows not what he speaks."

Perseus pushed himself away from the table and crossed the room to the window where he gazed out at the lone she-goat in the stone paddock. After a moment he said, "I know who my real father is now."

"*Do* you? Pray tell, who is he?"

"Someone named Proetus."

His mother looked at him. "Who told you that?"

"Dictys."

She pressed her lips together. "Dictys would be well advised to keep his mind on his fish and his nose out of other people's business."

"Then it's true?"

She rose from the table and went over to her son. "What else did Dictys tell you?"

"He said this Proetus was your uncle. Is that true too?"

"Proetus was my uncle."

"Well, that's just terrific! So I'm not only the man's son; I'm also his grandnephew. I'm both your son and your cousin, and I'm my own second cousin. Hell, I'm a whole extended family all by myself!"

Danae snorted. "You're the son of Zeus."

"Bullshit! I'm the son of some stupid old fart back in Argos."

"If you mean Proetus, he was no old fart, and he was anything but stupid."

Perseus turned to her, his eyes betraying both anger and curiosity. "What was he like, this Proetus?"

"He was dashing, with raven hair, and he wore a bronze sword that shined like the sun. He was thirty, and I was sixteen, and we wrestled in an olive grove on an early spring day when the air was as soft as the mossy ground."

Perseus turned away, squeamish to hear the details of his own conception. "So that was my father."

Danae shook her head. "You're the son of Zeus."

"Damn it, quit saying that!"

"But it's true. Work it out for yourself. You're twenty and I'm thirty-eight. That means I had you when I was eighteen. But I was with Proetus when I was sixteen. He went to Tiryns shortly after that, and I never saw him again. Do you really think a skinny wimp like you required a two-year gestation period?"

"Why should I believe you?"

"Because I never joke about my sex life. Besides, as I told you, Proetus had black hair just like mine. How likely is it that the two of us would have produced a blond child?"

"Oh, I see," he rejoined sarcastically. "So you're telling me Zeus has blond hair, right?"

Danae did not answer.

"Well, does he? If Zeus is my father, then you must have seen him. So what does the great 'King of the Gods' look like? You're not going to tell me he looks like that dumb old statue in the temple, are you?"

"No."

"Then what? What does he look like?"

"It's a little hard to say."

Perseus returned to the table and flopped back into a chair. From the dirt floor Danae lifted a jug of wine, sloshed it slightly to weigh its contents, then poured two earthen cups. She placed one in front of her son.

"I don't want any."

"Come on. Don't make me drink alone."

Gloomily he lifted the cup to his lips as his mother sat down across from him.

"Do you want to hear about it?" she asked.

"Hear about what?"

"The time Zeus came to me."

"I don't care."

"You'd better care, because I've never told the story to anyone, and I'll only tell it to you once."

* * *

"We may be poor now," Danae began, "and living on a godforsaken island ruled by a petty tyrant, but I was born a princess. My father, your grandfather, is Acrisius, King of Argos, and my mother, Aganippe, bore him only one child—me. Acrisius wanted a male heir, of course. All fathers do, but especially kings, so he traveled to the great oracle at Delphi to find out if he would ever have a son. After going into a trance, the priestess told him that he would have no more offspring, but worse than that, she told him that a grandchild of his—in other words, a child of mine—was destined to kill him.

"Well, the only sure way of keeping me from having children was to do away with me, but my father, for all his faults, couldn't do that. He did the next best thing, though. When he got back to Argos, he had a special chamber built in the courtyard of the palace, sunk into the earth. I was locked in, and the door was guarded at all times.

"The chamber was roomy, and he had provided it with everything I'd need, brought in my own bed and my other furniture so I'd be comfortable. He even had part of the roof removed and replaced with a brass grid so the sun could shine in. I'd just turned eighteen, though, and the thought of spending the rest of my life—or at least the rest of my father's life—locked underground was horrifying. But no one, not even my mother, would dare defy the king, so I cried a lot. I cried especially at night when the sun would slip below the horizon. Somehow the sunshine, passing freely through the grate, made it seem less like a prison. But at night the stars, cold and distant, seemed like fellow sufferers, each one twinkling a private message of despair from its own remote cell.

"Months passed, and then one evening around midnight while I was lying in my bed waiting for sleep to come, sleep being the only escape that I had, I became aware of light somewhere in the room. I thought at first that a servant had come with a torch, but the light didn't seem to be the glow of fire. It seemed too dispersed, too ... golden.

"From where I lay in my bed I could see the brass grid in the roof. Passing through it was a small cascade of tiny lights, little pinpricks of shining gold, like a miniature throng of fireflies descending through the bars. There were ten or twenty at first, and they hovered midway between the grate and the floor below, sparkling and glinting off other shiny objects in the chamber. Ten or twenty more joined them, and my eyes widened. Then, as if these were the scouts sent ahead to find the way, in a rush came all the rest, a whole shower of them, thousands and thousands of flickering lights pouring through the grid in a torrent and filling the room with gold.

"I sat up, wanting to scream but too terrified to utter a sound. The lights gathered together, and then as a rolling, glowing swarm they approached me. I burrowed back down under the covers, but the next moment they were upon me. The blanket was whipped away. I was pushed on my back by a living, golden waterfall. It overwhelmed me, enveloped me, entered me."

Mesmerized, Perseus sputtered, "Wh ... what happened then?"

"I passed out, I think."

He knitted his brows for several moments, then shook his head. "It was a dream."

"It was no dream."

"It had to be. I mean, come on, Mother, you don't really believe that Zeus came down as a shower of gold and then ..." He lowered his voice, not really wanting to utter the words. "And then ... made love to you, for God's sake."

Danae sneered. "Listen, o wise my son, who's never made love to anything more marvelous than his own right hand, I know what sex feels like and I know *where* it feels like. That sparkling shower knew exactly what it was doing, and if you don't think it was Zeus, then I'd like you to explain to me how I ended up with a scrawny little runt nine months later."

Perseus drummed his fingers on the table. "So what happened then? Did your father find out?"

"He would have. It's kind of hard to keep a crying baby secret for long, and you were one hell of a crybaby. My mother, in what was probably the most courageous act of her timid life, helped me to escape. She bribed the guard and smuggled us down to the harbor and onto a fishing boat—your friend Dictys' boat to be precise. And Dictys took us back home with him to Seriphos, the lovely island paradise where we now find ourselves."

Abruptly, Perseus rose from the table and trod back and forth in the small space of the room. "I don't understand. Why would Dictys lie about your uncle?"

"Oh, Dictys didn't really lie. He's just a gossipy old man who jumped to the wrong conclusion."

"And why, among all the women in the world, would Zeus choose you?"

"Maybe he already had all the others."

Perseus frowned. "I just can't believe an incredible story like that."

"Would you rather believe that you're your own cousin? Do stop pacing. You'll wear out your shoes, and I'll have to impose on the king's generosity to get you some new ones."

Stung, Perseus halted where he was and looked down helplessly at the floor.

"Sorry," she apologized. "Cheap shot." Danae went to him, hesitated, then put her arm around his waist. "Anyway, now I've told you. I don't care if you believe it or not. I've waited a long time to tell you that story."

"I'd like to believe you, Mother. I really would. But honestly, do I look like a son of Zeus? Tell me the truth."

She gave him a small squeeze. "You'd be surprised."

II
Messenger

FROM FAR DOWN THE BEACH Perseus recognized the stocky figure and grizzled beard of his friend. Dictys was plucking clumps of seaweed from the net and tossing them carelessly onto the sand. After a brief greeting, the two set to work hauling the net on shore, untwisting the tangled mesh and pulling it taut. Then, kneeling down under the intense Aegean sun, they began retying the strings that had broken in the swell, Perseus unusually quiet and Dictys humming a repetitive tune as he moved along. After about an hour Dictys commented, "I hear you're going to bring back Medusa's head for the king."

"News travels fast," Perseus said irritably.

"How do you intend to do it?"

"I don't intend to do it. I never intended to do it. There *are* no Gorgons, for God's sake. You don't believe in them, do you, Dictys?"

"I believe in them."

"Well, I don't. Tell me something: if there are such things as Gorgons, how come nobody's ever seen one, huh? How come nobody knows where they live?"

"I know where they live."

Perseus stopped what he was doing and looked at the old man. "You do?"

"Sure I do."

"Where do they live?"

"In the Land of the Hyperboreans."

"The Land of the Hyperboreans?" Perseus narrowed his eyes. "Where's that?"

"No idea."

Perseus turned his attention back to the net. "That's what I thought."

With difficulty, Dictys raised himself to his feet and pressed his fists into the small of his back as he stretched. "You know, you really shouldn't talk about them as if they're some whole species—'Gorgons'—like they're dogs or cats or some other damn fool animal."

"Well, aren't they? They're supposed to be a mythological beast, right?"

Dictys mopped his neck, then reached into his boat for a jug of water. After offering it to Perseus, who declined, he took a deep draft himself, and let a goodly amount of the cool liquid pour over his chest. "There are only three Gorgons," he said, "and they're human beings, or at least they used to be: Stheino, Euryale, and Medusa. Sisters, they were, and beautiful, especially Medusa. Lovely as a goddess, with long red hair, the color of fire. It was her hair, they say, that ensnared the great God of the Sea, Poseidon. It reminded him of flaming coral and, in the way it moved, the swirling eddies of the deep. Poseidon wanted Medusa, and one night when she came alone to Athena's temple to pray, he took her—right there on the temple floor."

"Hogwash," Perseus said under his breath.

"But this angered the goddess Athena," Dictys continued, unperturbed. "They'd desecrated her temple. She couldn't punish Poseidon, of course, so she took her revenge on Medusa instead— and on her sisters too, even though they had nothing to do with it. She turned all three of them into monsters, with claws and fangs and scaly wings like a dragon. But worst of all, remembering Medusa's gorgeous hair, Athena changed their locks into a mass of ugly, hissing snakes. So hideous did she make them that anyone who looks upon the face of a Gorgon is instantly turned to stone."

Perseus jerked the twine upward to tighten the last knot, then dropped the net and scrambled to his feet. "I'll see you tomorrow," he said over his shoulder as he headed down the shore.

"Wait." Dictys lifted a small basket of fish from the boat. "Don't forget this. Take it home to your mother."

* * *

"Turn people to stone!" Perseus muttered as he strode along the empty beach. He shifted the basket from one arm to the other. "What a bunch of gibberish. The gullibility of some people! If the sight of a Gorgon is supposed to turn anyone who looks at it to stone, then I'd like to know who the hell lived to describe it in such detail."

"Hey, that's good, Sport."

The words were spoken so close to his ear that Perseus started. A young man about his own age had fallen in step by his side.

Perseus stopped. "I ... I didn't see you. Where did you—"

"No, that's good," the other continued, paying no attention. "If a Gorgon turns anyone who looks at it to stone, then who lived to describe it? That's real good! It's like that old chestnut: if a tree falls in the woods and nobody's there, does it make a noise? It's a conundrum. I like conundrums almost as much as I like poetry, and

I *love* poetry."

The stranger was dressed as a Greek, but there was something different about his costume, something Perseus couldn't quite put his finger on. He spoke Greek too, but with an accent Perseus couldn't place, and his voice, though compelling, seemed oddly remote. Most peculiar of all, Perseus was sure he had never met him before; yet something about him seemed familiar.

"Do I know you?" Perseus asked.

"Only by reputation."

"What reputation?"

"I'm a member of that 'criminal pantheon' you mentioned earlier."

Perseus's eyes opened wide and the basket dropped from his hands, the slippery fish sliding out onto the sand.

"Hey, careful there, Sport," the stranger said, bending down to retrieve the fish. "Your mother's going to be pissed if you lose any of these." He refilled the basket and handed it back to Perseus, who took it mechanically. "Don't think I'm insulted, though, I mean about the 'criminal pantheon' crack. It's an apt description, when you think about it. Blunt, but apt. Besides, that's a great phrase: 'criminal pantheon.' Phraseology is everything. You can say whatever you want as long as you phrase it right. Don't you find that to be true? I mean, not all the time, of course, but most of the time?"

Perseus stared at him stupidly.

"Hey, Sport, you're going to have to be a little quicker than this if you expect to kill Medusa. I mean, I'll help you, for God's sake, but you're going to have to do most of it yourself."

Perseus swallowed hard. "Who are you?"

The stranger folded his arms, grinning. "Hermes. Son of Zeus; Messenger of the Gods; Guide to the Underworld; Night Wanderer; Patron of Thieves, Knaves, Travelers, and Pilgrims; Slayer of Argus; and general *Johannes factotum*."

Perseus shook his head. "No."

"No?"

"*No!* " he repeated more emphatically. Perseus turned his back and strode to one of the large stones littering the beach. He sat down deliberately.

"I am, you know," Hermes called after him. "Do you want me to do some magic to prove it? I can make that rock disappear so that you fall on your ass. Would that convince you?"

"No. I don't believe in you."

Hermes strolled over, planted his feet in front of Perseus, and eyed him for a few moments. "While you were helping Dictys with his nets before, you accidentally tied a granny knot, something you haven't done in years. You quickly undid it when his back was turned."

Perseus said nothing.

"This morning," Hermes continued, "when you went to get water from the well, you noticed that a small spider had already set up housekeeping in the bucket. You were about to drop the bucket, spider and all, into the water, but at the last minute while no one was looking, you coaxed the spider out."

Hermes tilted his head slightly, waiting for a response. When none was forthcoming, he went on. "Last night in bed, after you were sure your mother had fallen asleep, you—"

"Stop it!" Perseus shouted. "Damn you, stop it! You don't exist."

"Are you a betting man?"

"You *can't* exist. None of you gods can exist."

"Why not?"

"Because of all the stories about you. I can't believe that real gods would act like you do."

"What would real gods act like?"

"Real gods would be good, they'd be honest, they'd be fair."

"They'd be dull, dull as dishwater, Sport."

Perseus glared up at him. "We don't have gods to keep us

entertained. We have gods to set an example for us."

"An example of what?"

"Morality, for one thing."

"Ah, so that's it," Hermes said, nodding. "Why would you deny us pleasures of the flesh? We don't deny them to you."

"It's not that, but why don't you stick to your own kind?"

"Our own kind?"

"If you have to do it, for heaven's sake—and I don't see why gods have to do it in the first place—why can't you do it with ... goddesses?"

Hermes gave this some thought. "The field's just too narrow, Sport. Who do you suggest we bed down with? Herá, the wife of Zeus? Fat chance! Athena? She'd as soon stab you as look at you. The virgin goddess Artemis, perhaps, with her quiver of arrows? You'd end up looking like a pincushion."

"What about Aphrodite? She's supposed to be the Goddess of Love, isn't she?"

"Hell, everyone's already done it with Aphrodite half a dozen times."

"So you exploit mortal women instead."

"No more than mortal men do." Hermes smiled tolerantly, sat down next to him. "Listen, don't take it so much to heart. Whether you like us or not, or whether you approve of us or not, you've been singled out to receive our particular favor. This is your moment, Sport, your *annus mirabilis*, the epoch of your life that you're going to date everything from. You're about to embark on an adventure, and years from now you'll give anything you possess to relive a single minute of this time, but it'll never happen again if you live a hundred years. So savor it, Sport. You're now under the protection of the Olympian Gods."

As Hermes said this, he put his arm around his companion's shoulders, and at the first touch Perseus felt a prickling tingle run through every nerve of his body. It was something akin to goose bumps, or to the first flush of love, but it also had about it the morbid thrill of pain. His heart beat faster. There was a pounding in his temples, a clanging in his ears. What before had been a beach of sand and rocks and placid waves became a blinding white landscape lit by an exploding sun. With all his might, Perseus pulled away.

"Oh my God," he said, standing now and shaking on the sand. "You *are* a god."

"Bingo."

"Then it's all true."

"All true."

"Zeus came to my mother as a shower of gold."

"Yes, you're Zeus's son, same as me." Hermes leaned back on his hands and stretched out his legs on the warm rock. "We're half brothers, you might say. That would be a distinction, I guess, if I didn't have quite so many half brothers. Zeus gets around, as you may have heard."

"Oh my God."

"When you think about it, your mother fared pretty well. After all, a shower of gold doesn't seem so bad when you consider that Zeus came to Europa as a bull, and Europa, poor girl, was an ordinary woman, if you take my meaning."

"Oh my God."

"An appropriate exclamation, Sport, considering whom you're talking to, but the repetitive iteration is rendering it a bit moldy."

Perseus stared at him. "Then you know everything."

"Everything: past, present, and to come."

"And you're immortal. You'll live forever."

"I'll live forever, though I must admit, in rather straitened circumstances after a while, thanks to the Romans."

"The Romans?"

Hermes ambled over to the edge of the water. "Mirthless fellows who'll occupy a hip-boot-shaped peninsula west of here. They'll be second rate at just about everything they try, especially poetry. They won't hold a candle to your people. Their only talents will be in war and plumbing. So, needless to say, they'll be remarkably successful. They'll call me Mercury, of all things, after some petty local divinity, and I'll be ensconced in their official pantheon, to which all will pay homage, but in which none will believe. We Olympians will go into a long, slow decline with the Romans."

"They won't believe in you anymore?"

"No, and it gets worse. After the Romans, no one will even pay us lip service. No one but the poets. Ah, but the poets! They're worth all the rest. The poets will keep our names alive long after everyone thinks we never existed at all. Unfortunately, most of them will use our Roman names. Damn Romans spread their damn language everywhere."

Hermes picked up a small, flat stone. "There's one poet in particular that I love. He'll have a funny name and wear a funny ruff around his neck, but what a damn fine scribbler! Whenever he'll want to describe a man as swift, or nimble, or light on his feet, he'll compare him with me:

A station like the herald Mercury
New lighted on a heaven-kissing hill.

Isn't that great? Don't you think that captures me just right? 'New lighted on a heaven-kissing hill,' " he repeated, closing his eyes to savor the words. "He'll use me over and over again. Sometimes he'll call me by other names, but hell, it's obvious he's talking about me.

I'll put a girdle round about the earth
In forty minutes.

Now I ask you honestly, who else can do that but me?"

Hermes drew his arm back and let the stone fly. It took one high bounce off the surface of the water, then a second, half as high, a third, then finally degenerated into a series of small, rapid hops before slipping beneath the waves.

Perseus looked bewildered. "But why will people stop believing in you?"

"Competition."

"Competition? What kind of competition can—?" He eyed Hermes suspiciously. "Wait a minute. Some other gods must take your place. That's it, isn't it?"

"In a manner of speaking."

"And to supplant you, they must be better than you are: good and honest and fair."

"Well, that's a matter of opinion."

"And I'll bet they don't have human offspring."

"Don't be so sure about *that*." Hermes turned back from the shore. "But enough of comparative religion. We've got some work to do and not much time to do it. I've got to prepare you to meet the Gorgons."

"The Gorgons?"

"You promised the good king Medusa's head, and you're going to deliver."

"Then the Gorgons are for real?"

"Of course they're for real. Ugly bitches too."

"And I'm supposed to—"

"Sure. You want to save your mother from a fate worse than death, don't you? I mean, Polydectes isn't exactly a shower of gold."

"Yes, but—"

"That's why I'm here. Zeus sent me to help you."

"Why?"

"Why? Well, partly because he likes you. After all, you're his son, don't forget. Also, Zeus doesn't like to see someone else cut his grass, if you take my meaning."

"But how can I kill Medusa? I don't even know where she is or—"

"Hey, don't sweat the small stuff. Leave the details to me." Hermes put his hand on the young man's shoulder. Again Perseus felt the prickling sensation all the way to his extremities. "Trust me,

Sport. I'm the Slayer of Argus. I know how these things are done. Give me a little time, and I'll be back."

"But—"

Hermes began to walk up the beach. "They're going to compose an epic poem about you," he called over his shoulder. "A nice piece of work, divided into twenty-four books of choice dactylic hexameters. Not Homer, mind you, but decent verse nevertheless. Unfortunately," he added, "it'll be lost in the great fire of Alexandria. But at least they'll name a constellation after you."

"A constellation?"

"Don't let it go to your head. They're going to name one after Andromeda too."

"Who's And—"

"I go, I go; look how I go.
Swifter than arrow from Tartar's bow."

Hermes closed his eyes again. "Great, isn't he?"

Then Perseus was alone once more on the deserted beach.

III
Gifts of the Gods

"How did the fish get all full of sand?" Danae asked irritably, peering into the basket.

"I dropped them. Listen, Mother, the strangest thing—"

"You dropped them," she repeated dryly. "I've got to sleep with the ugliest man on Seriphos, and you drop the fish in the sand."

"Mother, you may not have to—"

"Oh, I hope to Zeus he doesn't have bad breath." She lifted one of the fish and poured water over it, then flopped the long, slippery form on a wooden block. "He will, though. I know he will. Ugh! That's going to be the worst part of it." Danae paused, a cleaver in her right hand. "Well, the second worst part." She chopped off the head.

"*Mother.*"

"What is it?"

Perseus hesitated. "I ... might be going away for a while."

She turned to him. "Going away? Where?"

"I don't know exactly."

"You don't know. Well, that's just wonderful! It's not bad enough that I've got to become the concubine of a little tinhorn despot, but you, the only worthless son I have, are going to go off and leave me here alone. Is this something you cooked up with Dictys? Are you going on his boat? I've got a good mind to—"

"Dictys has nothing to do with it."

Danae drew closer to her son and scrutinized his features. "Why are you leaving me?"

"There might be a way to avoid ..."

"Avoid what?"

"The king, Polydectes."

She narrowed her eyes. "How?"

He did not respond.

Danae's stern demeanor did not alter, but when she spoke again, her voice had moderated. "Perseus, I know what you're thinking of doing, but I want you to put it out of your mind. People have tried to resist Polydectes before. He's got spies everywhere, and it's the first thing he'll suspect if you try to leave the island. He'll have you followed. With no friends you can trust, no relations, you'll be an easy mark for him." She sighed. "Listen, I shouldn't have made such a big fuss over it. It wasn't your fault, and it won't be so bad. Besides, after a while he'll get tired of me and—"

"Damn it, you're not going to sleep with that stinking slob!"

Danae was taken aback. Her face softened. "Don't think I don't appreciate this, Perseus, because I do. I know you want to help, but there's nothing you can do. Do you understand me? Nothing."

"What makes you so sure?"

"I'm sorry, Perseus. It's just that I know you. You're a good boy, and you mean well, but you're not ..."

"I'm not *what*?" he demanded.

"You're not a hero."

* * *

Perseus woke in the early morning twilight. His initial thought, even before he remembered the strange events of the previous day, was to get water from the well, the first of his daily chores. He groped in the darkness for his shoes, but his hand fell upon something unfamiliar next to his bed. A bag of some sort, a leather bag. Curious, he snatched it up and padded barefoot through the darkened room and out into the air.

A few of the brightest stars still shone, but they were rapidly fading in the cool, gray light of morning. From behind the low stone wall the she-goat watched him cross the yard. Absently, Perseus patted the goat's hard head, then leaned his back against the gatepost while he examined the strange pouch in his grasp. It was larger than a wineskin, with a drawstring at the mouth that was pulled snugly and tied in a knot. He lifted it a couple of times to judge its weight. There was something inside, but of no considerable mass. Perplexed, he looked around the yard as if to seek the rightful owner, but no one was there except the she-goat, who looked at him blankly through the odd, rectangular pupils of her eyes.

Perseus slid down to a seated position on the ground with the bag on his lap. After carefully untying the knot, he spread open the mouth and reached inside. He thought at first that he had found his shoes.

They certainly felt like shoes. Perhaps his mother had seen them lying about somewhere and left them here for him, but why would she put them in a bag? Then it occurred to him that Danae might have already prevailed on the king's generosity, just as she had threatened to do the day before, and this was Polydectes' first gift to the family. The idea repelled him. Roughly, he pulled the shoes out and tossed the bag away.

For a while his theory seemed plausible. They were a new pair of sandals and of the type that might indeed be a royal gift. Made of fine, supple leather, with delicate workmanship, they were too open, too light for a common person. The first time he tried to scramble up a rock pile, the fragile straps would probably break from the strain. Or the first mud he trod through might suck them right off his feet. No, they were useless to Perseus except to remind him of the shame his mother had gone through to obtain them. He was just about to heave them in the same direction as the bag when he noticed the wings.

Attached to the sides of each heel and tapering backward was a diminutive pair of wings made of the same pliable material as the sandals themselves. Gingerly, Perseus fingered one of them, then dropped the sandals with a start. The wing had fluttered in his hand.

"Try them on, Sport."

Perseus's head snapped up.

Hermes was bending over to retrieve the leather bag from the ground. "And don't lose this, for God's sake. This is what you're going to put Medusa's head in." Hermes tossed it into his lap. "Tie it to your belt."

Mechanically, Perseus obeyed, then looked down at the strange winged sandals again. "What *are* these?"

"What do they look like? You didn't expect to go halfway around the world in those disgraceful old gunboats of yours, did you? I've done you a favor and burned them."

"You burned my shoes?"

"Come on, try on your new footgear. If you like them, I'm thinking of coming out with a whole line of them. 'Hermes Cloud-Hoppers.' What do you think? I'll put my logo on them and really clean up."

"But I don't understand. What are the wings for?"

"Oh, just a little bit of whimsy on my part. The sandals would have functioned just as well without them, but hell, what would life be without a few dramatic flourishes, right? So go ahead: try them on."

Dubiously, Perseus eyed the tiny wings that seemed to have a life of their own, but he slipped one of the sandals on, winding the long straps around his calf and tying them below his knee. Feeling nothing peculiar except the usual sensation of new shoes, he slipped on the second, tied it, then rose to his feet.

"How do they fit?"

"They fit all right."

Hermes crouched down now and adjusted the sandals slightly, feeling Perseus's heel and pressing on the leather band over his instep. "You'll have to expect a little tightness at first until you break them in."

"They fit fine."

"Plenty of toe room?"

"They're fine!" he repeated impatiently. "But I don't think they're very practical."

"Why not?"

"They're too ... flimsy."

"Flimsy? What are you talking about? These are made of the finest grain cowhide, hand stitched."

"I know, I know, but I just don't think I'd be able to walk very far in them."

Hermes straightened up now and flashed a sly grin. "Who said anything about walking? Look at your feet, Sport."

Perseus glanced down and saw nothing unusual, nothing but the new sandals themselves. He was about to look up again when he noticed the shadows. The sun had risen over the horizon now and was casting long shadows in the yard. Hermes had one, and Perseus another, but there was a difference between the two. Hermes' shadow began at the very spot where his feet touched the ground, but the shadow Perseus cast began some distance away from his feet, leaving a patch of sunlight directly below him. It was almost as if his feet weren't on the ground at all, but were hovering a few inches in the—

"Oh my God," Perseus exclaimed. As he tried to put his feet back down on the ground, he only succeeded in raising them still higher in the air. He kicked vigorously, and the next thing he knew, his feet had flipped completely over his head, as if he'd been caught in the undertow of the surf. The only difference was that instead of crashing back down to the ground, he found himself sailing, upside down, over the stone paddock. The she-goat, chewing tranquilly, watched him as he glided by.

"Hey, Sport, the idea is to go forward, not backward."

Perseus flailed helplessly, doing a series of graceless aerial somersaults. With each revolution of his body, he folded his arms over his head, fearing a plunge to earth that would crack his skull, but he did not seem to be able to fall. Instead, he continued to tumble recklessly through the air and fly farther away from the yard.

"Don't let them control you," Hermes shouted. "You've got to control *them*."

But Perseus continued to pitch and roll randomly. If there were any constant at all in his haphazard progress, it was the perverse tendency of his head to remain lowermost in the configuration of his body. This attitude caused the world to appear upside down. It also caused him to feel sick.

"Concentrate," Hermes exhorted. "You've got to concentrate."

Closing his eyes and gritting his teeth, Perseus tried with all his might to stop moving, to wrest control of his legs from the capricious little wings. Eventually his speed did seem to slacken. The wind that had been rushing by his face calmed until it was little more than the gentle morning breeze.

"That's the idea. You've got it now, Sport. All you've got to do is turn around and come back."

Perseus began to wheel slowly to one side, and as he did so, he opened his eyes again. The first thing he saw was the roof of his own home forty feet below, and nothing standing between him and it but the vacant air. Panic seized him, and he whirled violently, sending himself flying again, but this time back toward the yard. Hermes winced and covered his eyes.

Tumbling uncontrollably in the direction of the paddock, Perseus saw the gatepost looming in his path. He reached out for it, crashed his shoulder into it, but managed to snag it anyway. Then by an odd sort of inverted climbing he hauled himself back to earth again. Never letting go of the rough wood, he scrambled to his knees just in time to unceremoniously empty the contents of his stomach onto the ground.

"Needs a little work, Sport."

IV
Directives

IN A REMOTE COVE and with the help of a long rope, Hermes gave
Perseus flying lessons. After several hours Perseus still did not look
particularly graceful when airborne, but Hermes concluded that he
had at least achieved sufficient mastery over the winged sandals
to get where he needed to go. He broke off the instruction and sat
Perseus down.

"Do you know any geography?" Hermes asked.

"No."

"Well, at least you're honest." With a stick he drew a crude map
in the sand. "Okay, lookee here. This is Seriphos, where we are right
now." He poked the stick at a small circle. "To the west over here
is mainland Greece, where you and your mother came from. To the
east is Asia, and down here south of you is Africa. Got that?"

"Yes."

"Now, if you were an ace pilot—which you're not—I'd have

you fly straight south over the water this way, see? But I don't think we ought to take that chance. You're liable to end up in the drink. So I'm going to have you do some island hopping eastward, this way," he said, bouncing the tip of the stick across the sand, "and then take the coastline down. That way if you need to stop for a rest, you can. Also, you're less likely to get lost. See what I mean?"

"But where am I going?"

"Here." He traced his stick all the way down the eastern edge of Africa nearly to the bottom and planted it in a large island off the coast.

"How far away is that?"

"Oh, five thousand miles, as the crow flies."

"*Five thousand miles!* "

"Give or take a furlong."

"And that's the Land of the Hyperboreans?"

"Hell, no. What gave you that idea? That's in the opposite direction. This is Cimmeria."

"Why am I going *there*?"

"To see the Gray Women."

"What Gray Women?"

"The 'Graeae' is their proper name, but who can pronounce 'Graeae,' right? They're sisters, two old crones who haven't got two eyes between them—literally. They share this one bloodshot peeper by passing it back and forth when there's something worth looking at. You're going to steal that eye."

"What do I need another eye for?"

"You don't need the eye, Sport. You're just stealing the eye so that they'll give you the Cap of Invisibility. You'll make an exchange, see? They stole the cap to begin with, so they can't kick too much about losing it. But you'll need it to be able to approach the Gorgons. Get the picture now? Once the Gray Women give you the cap, you can return the eye."

Perseus fumed. "This is absurd. Who would think up such a

complicated, pointless escapade? You're a god: if I'm supposed to have this cap, why can't you just go get it for me like you did these damn sandals? Why should I waste my time going five thousand miles out of my way?"

"You're not catching on, Sport. If you want to take part in an epic adventure, you've got to play by the rules."

"I *don't* want to take part. I *never* wanted to take part."

"But you do want to save your mother from Polydectes, don't you?"

He set his jaw. "Yes."

"There you are, then. Besides, there'll be some benefits in it for you. Trust me. You'll see."

Perseus examined the map again. "So how do I find these Gray Women once I get to Cimmeria?"

"Glad you asked." Hermes pointed with the stick. "Facing the outer ocean is a reef three hundred miles long. Behind the reef, three rivers drain from the coast into the sea. If you follow the middle one, it will lead you to its source high up on the plateau. You'll find the Gray Women in an abode where the sun never shines."

"Terrific," Perseus muttered.

"Now the only way you can steal the eyeball is to sneak up on them and snatch it while they're passing it from one to the other. And don't underestimate them. They may look like harmless old biddies, but if one of them sees you coming, you're history, so be careful."

Perseus pulled himself to his feet and ambled down to the water. "Even if I get this cap, how am I supposed to approach the Gorgons if I can't look at them?"

"We're still working on that one, Sport, but don't worry. We'll think of something by the time you're ready."

"And how am I supposed to kill Medusa anyway? I don't even have a weapon."

"That problem we *have* taken care of."

Perseus turned around. Hermes was gone, but he had left something behind. Stuck in the sand—off the map, as it were, or perhaps in the featureless north that Hermes had not filled in—was a bronze sword that shined like the sun.

* * *

A string of six islands separated Seriphos from the coast of Asia Minor. As he stood alone on the beach early the next morning, Perseus could see the first of them, Siphnos, a gray mound to the southeast, partly shrouded by the morning mists. He was dressed in his best tunic, which was of the same rough cloth as his worst but had fewer rents. He'd thrust the bronze sword in his belt. In the leather bag that was meant for Medusa's head, he'd stowed some bread and cheese for his journey. On his feet were the winged sandals, which even now betrayed their unruly intelligence, fluttering, anxious to propel him on his way.

He took a last look around. Though his mother had told him he was born in Argos and had been brought here as an infant, he had never known any other home but this island, and he had never set foot off it except to go fishing on Dictys' boat. His entire knowledge of the outside world had come in the form of fantastic stories, most of which he hadn't believed. After the events of the last two days, he no longer knew what to believe. He picked up a handful of the sand and rubbed it into his palms.

The ghostly gray mass rose out of the water far in the distance. Perseus took a deep breath, held it for a moment, then bent his knees and leapt into the air.

"Think of flying as a notion, Sport," Hermes had advised him. "Not a belief, mind you. That's way too solid, too heavy. That'll never fly. And not a fancy either, because a fancy is too light. It'll run away with you. Leave fancy to the poets. No, think of flying as just a notion, something you might change, shift positions on, something you wouldn't assert too strongly, something you can pick up or put down as the spirit moves you. Think of it that way, Sport, and you'll fly."

And so Perseus flew. A hundred feet below him on this misty, early summer's morning, the wine dark Aegean rolled beneath a new creature of the air.

Hermes had cautioned him about the cold. No matter how mild the temperature might be on the ground, the higher Perseus flew, the chillier he would be. Consequently, Perseus had worn a thick woolen mantle over his tunic, and under ordinary circumstances he might indeed have shivered a bit this high up, but a man flying is no ordinary circumstance.

Once airborne for a while, Perseus found he could ignore the recurrent bouts of terror at doing what no earthbound creature was meant to do. He began to enjoy the experience, especially the wind. He delighted in the way it blew through his hair and made his clothing billow. He undid several fastenings of his cloak so that it streamed out behind him as in pictures of the gods. He discovered that he could also use the wind to change direction, to bank with his body so as to swerve left or right, as a swimmer does in the water. He practiced some tolerable figure eights. He tried to go faster too, and quickly realized that he could increase his speed by assuming a horizontal posture and maintaining as narrow a profile as possible. He tried holding both arms at his side, then stretched them both out in front of him, then held one out and the other tucked close to his ribcage.

So absorbed did he become in his experimentation that he nearly overshot his mark. All of a sudden Siphnos loomed beneath him.

He'd already learned that the hardest part of flying was landing, and the hardest part of landing was slowing down. Perseus chose an isolated section of shore, then banked his body to present as wide a resistance to the wind as possible, while at the same time restraining the influence of the tiny wings. Nevertheless, he came in too fast and avoided a nasty collision only through a stumbling run along the beach. Shaking, but still on his feet when he finally came to a stop,

Perseus took a quick mental inventory to make sure all parts of him were sound. Then, relieved, he allowed his knees to buckle and sat cross-legged right where he was.

The shore looked familiar. The white sand running through his fingers, the sun-baked rocks, the multicolored pebbles beneath the clear, brilliant blue water were indistinguishable from those he'd left behind. Indeed, the two isles were as similar as their two names, Siphnos and Seriphos. Perseus might be sitting on his own beach, but in fact he was not. Though a mere ten miles away, he had traveled that distance as no human being ever had before.

Out of breath, scared to be leaving home, apprehensive about what was in store, and lonely already, Perseus nevertheless looked back across the water at the island he'd left behind, and an odd, crooked grin crinkled his face.

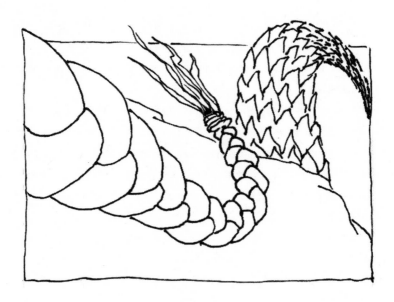

V
Damsel

AFTER ISLAND HOPPING all the rest of the day, Perseus reached the coast by evening. In a small wood not far from the beach he made an impromptu camp and prepared to spend the night under the stars. He found he had little appetite for the food he'd brought along, and when the sun went down and he stretched out on the ground, his woolen cloak for a blanket, he had trouble falling asleep. The tread of forest creatures through the twigs, the calls of night birds, the sound of foreign wind whispering through foreign trees kept him long awake. He thought more than once of his mother, who was also sleeping alone on this, his first night away from home.

In the morning Perseus headed south. Over land now instead of water, he was able to stop whenever he wanted, but he required little rest. Prudently he flew higher than before, since he encountered more cities along the coast. Yet he couldn't help slowing to marvel at what he saw. Great mountain ranges rippled on the inland horizon. Vast, cultivated fields filled the plains, and below him were bustling harbor towns, their docks busy with ships and activity, people moving from place to place like nervous ants. He was not only seeing things he had never seen before, but he was observing them from a perspective only the gods enjoyed.

By the fourth day Perseus had reached the coast of Phoenicia. He stuck close to the shoreline and flew the entire morning without a stop, then spied out a rocky cliff as a suitable place for his midday meal. The cliff faced the sea, and its sheer sides discouraged human traffic, but halfway up was a long, narrow shelf, ideal for an hour's respite.

Perseus had landed many times by now and had gained in both confidence and expertise. He had even begun to take a modest pride in his skill. He slowed as he descended, bent his knees, ready to absorb the impact, but just as his feet began to scrape the pebbles on the surface, he started. At the far end of the ledge was the nude figure of a woman.

Flustered but unable to abort his landing, Perseus staggered into the rock wall, banging his arm. He fell backward while still in motion, slid on his buttocks along the ledge until he came to an undignified halt just inches from her.

Slender and about Perseus's age, she had been reclining upon an outcrop of stone, her head facing away from him. Her thick, brown hair was pulled into long side braids, their ends falling over the side of the rock like two lengths of auburn rope. The slanting, hard surface did not readily accommodate repose, and she had steadied herself only by keeping one knee bent so that she could brace the sole of her foot against the rock. Startled by his clumsy arrival, the young woman now leapt to her feet.

With some difficulty Perseus raised himself up again and backed a few steps away, unconsciously rubbing his bruised arm. It was only now that he noticed the chain. She gripped it tightly in her left hand, but her grasp was superfluous, for the chain was fastened to a manacle around her wrist. The other end was attached to a ring hammered into the living rock. Fettered as she was, any attempt at modesty would have been altogether futile. Therefore she covered herself only by the stern look she directed at the intruder.

Gallantry dictated that Perseus avert his eyes, for she was clearly helpless. Yet he seemed singularly unable to do so. In fact, he gaped openly. Except for representations of goddesses, Perseus had never seen a naked woman before. The immortals were always pictured full-breasted and full-hipped, but this girl had very slim hips and hardly any breasts at all. Indeed, at first he might have taken her for a boy.

The young woman grew visibly annoyed at his scrutiny. She arched an eyebrow. "*Well?*"

Startled, but still preoccupied, Perseus sputtered, "You ... don't have much of a chest."

The hostility in her features was replaced momentarily by bafflement. She glared. "Neither do you." She had intensely brown eyes, that shade of brown so deep it approaches black. "Who *are* you?" she demanded.

"My name is Perseus. Who are you?"

"Andromeda."

"Andromeda," he repeated. "I've heard that name before."

"I've heard that *line* before."

"What are you doing up here?"

"I could ask you the same question."

"Me? I just stopped to rest," he explained.

"Oh, really? You just stopped to rest on a rock ledge inaccessible from below and reached from above only by means of a rope. Tell me another one." Andromeda eyed him suspiciously. "Phineus sent you!"

"Phineus?"

"Yes, of course, that's it. It's got to be Phineus. You're supposed to rescue me, and then I'm supposed to be eternally grateful to him." She looked Perseus up and down, noting his tattered clothing.

"Where on earth did he drag you up from? He sure isn't trying to impress me with the splendor of his champion."

"Who is this Phineus?"

"Didn't he tell you? He's my uncle, my father's brother. He's also my fiancé, my betrothed, my intended."

"Your *uncle*?" Perseus repeated grumpily. "I don't get it. I just don't understand what the big attraction is between women and their damned uncles."

"Well, in my case, no attraction at all. Phineus is a disgusting old rascal. He lost most of his teeth and all of his sense in drunken brawls, and you can tell him I said so."

"Then why do you want to marry him?"

"Who said anything about wanting to? Phineus has a sizeable estate, and consequently a sizeable following. My father is the king, and he figures marrying his brother to me is the best way to keep a rein on him."

"That's unconscionable!"

Andromeda seemed amused. "Unconscionable? That's odd coming from you. If you've got a conscience, why are you working for Phineus?"

"I'm not working for Phineus. I don't even know anyone named Phineus."

"Then what are you doing here?"

"I'm ... on my way somewhere."

"Oh, right. I forgot. And you stopped here for a snooze. So where are you on your way to?"

He hesitated. "Cimmeria."

Andromeda laughed.

"What's so funny? That *is* where I'm going."

"Yes, and I'm going to the moon. Cimmeria, dear boy, is at the edge of the world. No one goes there. Here I thought you were just one of Phineus's stooges, and it turns out you're a lunatic instead."
She laughed again.

Angered but unwilling to debate his itinerary with her, Perseus turned to leave. After a few steps, he stopped suddenly, drew his sword, and strode toward her again.

The laughter died on Andromeda's lips, and she winced as Perseus lifted the bronze over her head. The next sound she heard was the clang of metal on metal as the chain that had pinioned her to the wall snapped in two. When she opened her eyes again, she raised her left hand in front of her, free now except for the ponderous bracelet and dangled links.

Once more Perseus began to leave.

"Wait," Andromeda called to him. "It won't do any good."

He spun around. "What won't do any good?"

"Freeing me. I can't get out of here, and even if I could, they'd just chain me back up again."

"Who would?"

"My parents."

"Your parents? Why would your parents do this to you?"

She fell silent, gazing down at her nakedness. Her face betrayed not shame, but a look of annoyed resignation.

Perseus hesitated, then heaved a sigh and undid the clasp on his cloak.

* * *

"So why did they chain you up? Because you didn't want to marry your uncle?"

Andromeda pulled the rough wool of Perseus's mantle more tightly around her. "No. That had nothing to do with it. I'm here to be sacrificed to the sea serpent."

"Sea serpent?"

She stretched, enjoying the freedom of movement again. She walked the full length of the narrow ledge and back again, working her sore wrist the while. "My mother is Cassiopeia. She's very beautiful. You'd like her: big bosom and everything. She has an ugly streak of vanity though, and one day she made the mistake of comparing her looks to the Nereids. Do you know the Nereids?"

"They're supposed to be some kind of mermaids."

"Sea nymphs, daughters of Nereus, one of the Immortals. Anyway, Nereus got wind of what my mother said. To teach her a lesson he's sent a sea serpent to Joppa every day right before sunset, and the serpent's been devouring villagers. The people demanded that my father do something about it, so he consulted an oracle. He was told that if no one was able to kill the serpent, the only way he could appease Nereus was to sacrifice either his wife or his daughter to it. Guess who he chose."

"You mean your mother's letting you die in her place?"

"Are you going to tell me that's unconscionable too?" She yawned, stretched again. "They gave me a great sendoff last night in the palace. You should have seen it: banquet, music, entertainment—the works."

"That was big of them. And now you're just content to die?"

"Well, at least I won't have to marry Phineus."

"Hasn't anyone tried to kill the serpent?"

"What are you imagining? A little garden snake? The thing's thirty feet long if it's an inch. My father offered a sizeable reward, but so far nobody's volunteered for the honor." She glanced up at the sun, which was past meridian. "If you stay around here a few more hours, you'll get a real close view of it. I suggest you leave whatever way you came."

Frowning, Perseus stood for a moment in thought, then abruptly took hold of her. "Come on."

"Come on where?"

"I'm getting you out of here."

"How? Do you have a rope?"

"I don't need a rope. Hold on to me."

When Perseus slipped his arm around her waist, attempting to draw her close, she pushed him away. "What do you think you're doing?"

"I'm trying to get you off this ledge, and I can't do it unless you hold on to me."

"I've heard a lot of dumb ploys in my time, but I've got to hand it to you, Perseus. Yours is the dumbest."

"Listen, don't flatter yourself. You're not my type. If you don't want me to help you, then the hell with you. You can just stay here and get eaten for all I care."

Dubiously, she stepped up behind him and put both arms around his chest, locking her hands. "All right, Hotshot, I'm holding on to you. What's supposed to happen now?"

* * *

"Oh my God!" she shrieked.

"Which way is the palace?" Perseus asked over his shoulder as he tried to fly steadily with Andromeda clinging to him.

"Oh my God! Oh my God!"

"Will you loosen up a little? I can't breathe. Which way is the palace?"

"Are you a god?"

"Yes, so you'd better answer me."

"That way." She began to point, which caused her to lose her grip. As she slipped, she snatched at Perseus again and in the process tugged the sparse hairs that grew on his chest. Perseus cried out in pain.

"You're no god!" Andromeda shouted.

"Congratulations."

"So how can you fly?"

"By thinking of it as a notion. Is there a place where I can land near the palace without being seen?"

"There's a walled garden out in back. What do you want to go to the palace for?"

"To see the king. Can you arrange it?"

"Why should I?"

"Because if you won't, I'll drop you."

VI
Joppa

WORD OF THE PRINCESS'S RETURN spread quickly through the palace, and when a hasty audience with the king was convened, the meeting chamber was filled to capacity. As he stood in the center of the hall with Andromeda, Perseus gazed at the elegant surroundings and all the grand personages lining the walls. This was nothing like Polydectes' homely court back on Seriphos. Unused to such splendor, Perseus became painfully aware of his appearance, his torn tunic, his shaggy hair.

A door opened, and immediately the murmuring around the room ceased as all heads bowed to the King and Queen of Joppa. They made a formal procession through the chamber, then mounted a draped platform on which stood two equal thrones. In his late forties King Cepheus cut an impressive figure. His clothes rich and well tailored, his mustache meticulously trimmed, he held himself as one who knew he deserved the royal title he bore. For all his grandeur, though, there was a curious blandness about him, as if he were ill-cast in the storied role of king. In another age he might have found a more comfortable if less romantic niche in the upper reaches of a large corporate stratosphere. By far the more interesting person was the woman whose hand rested lightly upon his arm.

Cassiopeia was darkly beautiful. Her black eyes her daughter might have inherited, but her shocking black hair she shared with no one. It fell in a cascade of raven spirals and ringlets on her bare shoulders. Her womanly figure was scarcely concealed by the close-fitting gown she wore. Yet her seductiveness was as much in her expression as in her form, its beguilement at once alluring and terrifying.

With a swirl of robes, the royal couple took their seats. After briefly sizing up the poorly dressed, blond stranger, the king spoke in calm, measured tones. "Young man—Perseus," he added significantly, pronouncing the name with care to show that he had made a point of learning it. "Through our daughter, so unexpectedly returned to us, you have sought this urgent interview, and we have acceded to your request. Under normal circumstances in a case such as this, we would be called upon to perform the happy duty of welcoming you to Joppa and of thanking you, both in our speech and in more tangible ways, for the inestimable service you performed in rescuing our child. Heaven knows, as everyone in this room surely knows, there is nothing we would like better in the world than to reward your service and receive our Andromeda back in our court again."

Cepheus paused to allow his statements thus far to be digested, then furrowed his brow to show the gravity of what was to follow. "Unfortunately, as all here know to our own sorrow, circumstances at present are anything but normal. Our land is afflicted by a sore menace of which you have heard, I believe."

Perseus made a quick nod.

"Good," the king said, nodding also and pursing his lips to show that he and the young man had already reached some understanding together. "Good," he repeated. "Then you may discern our intolerable ambivalence at seeing our daughter again. On the one hand we rejoice to have her in our midst, a pleasure that none of us had hoped for. On the other hand we grieve anew at the terrible loss we must sustain, for it is only by means of her unselfish sacrifice that our land can be preserved. That sacrifice unperformed, the commonwealth remains forfeit and in direst peril."

Cepheus gently put his fingertips together. "So you see, Perseus, your act, brave though it was and smacking of admirable youthful temerity, has nevertheless thwarted the lamentable but necessary oblation laid upon us. Though we weep yet again at the loss of a precious member of our family, dear to us as one of our own limbs, we must sadly embrace that loss and return her to the rock from whence you delivered her. Only by this means may our community persist, whole and entire."

Cepheus fell silent now and settled back in his throne, indicating by these signs that he would hear a response. The assembly, one and all, turned their attention from the king to the ill-clad young man.

Whatever Perseus had intended to say, he'd long since forgot. Cowed by his surroundings and by the king's eloquence, Perseus shrank from the idea of revealing his own rude speech. He would have preferred to sink beneath the floor and disappear.

After a brief, uncomfortable interval, Cepheus formed his lips into a tolerant smile and said, "Speak, Perseus."

But Perseus remained mute.

"Listen, you idiot," Andromeda hissed, "you made me set this up. You'd better say something."

When several moments had passed and Perseus still had not spoken, the king raised his chin slightly, taking in the entire assembly. "Well," he intoned, "it's a wise man, they say, who knows when to hold his peace."

There was a small ripple of indulgent laughter in the hall.

Perseus looked around at the assembled nobility, who were smiling condescendingly at him. Up on the platform the king, pleased no doubt with the outcome of this audience, chatted with his wife. Andromeda, still wrapped in the rough cloak, the chain dangling from her wrist, looked down at the floor. Perseus felt his lips quiver, and in his brain he heard a voice, his mother's voice: "You're the son of Zeus."

King Cepheus rose now, betokening the end of the audience. As he did so, Perseus blurted out, "You offered a reward."

Startled, the king raised an eyebrow. "No, young man, you've misunderstood me. As I said, there can be no reward for rescuing our daughter, since—"

"I don't mean for that," Perseus broke in. "I mean for killing the serpent."

The bland smile returned as Cepheus resumed his seat. "Yes, a reward was offered, but no one—"

"Is it still offered?"

Unused to being interrupted, the king paused, but his smile did not fade. Rather he displayed it to the rest of the assembly to show that he was not offended and was willing to indulge someone so unfamiliar with courtly manners. "Yes, it's still offered. Do you mean to collect it?"

"No. I don't want the reward. But if I kill the serpent, will you give me your daughter instead?"

Andromeda's head snapped up, and gasps were heard from several quarters. The king, his features suddenly menacing, was just about to speak when he felt his wife's hand on his arm.

"Perseus, you must forgive our dismay," she said in a low, caressing voice. "It is merely because you have surprised us. We had no idea that you loved our Andromeda." Cassiopeia smiled placidly at her daughter, but her black eyes betrayed something else. "Andromeda is a princess, as you know."

"I know."

"Do not misunderstand me. I say this not to remind you of your different social ranks, for such differences would of course be erased by your destruction of the serpent."

Startled, Cepheus turned to the queen, but she squeezed his arm.

"Rather I remind you of Andromeda's position merely to gain your assurance that, should we agree to your terms and should you prevail, you will proceed honorably with our daughter and accept her as nothing less than your lawful wife."

Andromeda glared up at her mother.

"I understand," Perseus responded.

Cassiopeia leaned over now and conferred quietly with her husband, who pressed his lips together and nodded several times. Finally he stood up.

"Perseus," he said, "we have considered your proposal. We admire your courage no less than your forthrightness, and in the interest of fair play, we have decided to accept your offer. If you kill the serpent—and the most high Zeus grant that you may—we agree to give you our daughter to wife. So for one and for all, young man, we wish you good luck and Godspeed."

As the king and queen departed, Perseus whispered to Andromeda. "That was easier than I thought it would be."

"Dunce!" she responded. "They only agreed to it because they know you're going to die."

* * *

Gulls cried overhead. From his seat on the broad rock, Perseus glanced up at them, then quickly resumed his vigil. This was the place where the serpent always came ashore, Andromeda had told him, right at the foot of the cliff where she had been chained. Before he'd left the palace, she had sent him to the kitchen to be fed—a "last meal" she called it. Dressed in her own chiton again, she had returned his cloak and accompanied it with the assurance that he was a fool for throwing his life away. Now as he sat alone on the beach, he wondered if she was right.

Low in the west, the sun shone on the water, making it difficult for him to discern things on the shifting, fluid surface. More gulls cried, and he ignored them, but as they became louder and more frenzied, he looked upward again only to glimpse a crust of bread ascending. One of the birds swooped down and snatched it in midair, the others screaming in protest. Perseus spun around and saw Hermes breaking a fragment from the loaf. He tossed this skyward also, aiming it at a small, mottled bird, but a large white one intercepted the morsel and gobbled it down.

"Greedy beggars, aren't they?" Hermes commented. "They don't care jack beans about anybody else, only themselves. That's what I like about gulls: pure selfishness. Nothing more reliable on Zeus's green earth. I think the major cause of trouble in the world is people wanting to do good unto others."

Hermes thrust the loaf back into the leather bag and dropped it behind the rock where Perseus had left it. "Take you, for instance," he continued, sitting down by Perseus's side. "Now what business have you got meddling in the internal affairs of Joppa?"

Perseus turned away and did not answer.

"Is it the girl?"

"No, it's the principle."

"Principles are the *second* major cause of trouble in the world."

"What are you doing here?" Perseus asked irritably.

"What am *I* doing here? I could be asking *you* that. You should've been halfway to Cimmeria by now. Hell, you weren't even supposed to meet Andromeda until you were on your way home. Now your chroniclers are going to get it all wrong. You've got to get with the program, Sport."

"I've got something to take care of first."

Hermes looked out at the water. "Seen any sign of him yet?"

"No."

"He's a *big* bastard, I hear."

"I know."

"Poisonous too. He grazes you with his choppers and you're dead meat." Hermes squinted. "Hey, what's that out there?"

"Where?" All alert, Perseus sat up, straining to see where his companion was pointing.

"There. See it?"

Perseus relaxed, shook his head. "Driftwood."

"Oh." Hermes leaned back on the rock. "I was watching you back there at the court. Didn't you love King Cepheus? I could listen to him for hours. Pure politician. Smoo-ooth! That man can make horseshit sound like a fruit salad. And his wife! What a looker! I wouldn't mind polishing her silver."

"I didn't notice."

Hermes snorted, then patted the other's knee and stood up. "Okay, Sport. I'm off."

Perseus was startled. "You're not going to stay?"

"Hell, no. I'm supposed to help you get the Gorgon's head—that's all. If you want to waste your time making the world safe for democracy, you're going to have to do it on your own."

"All right then, go!" Perseus snapped.

As Hermes strolled up the beach, he called over his shoulder, "I'll give you a tip, though. He's a myopic son of a bitch."

"Who is?"

"The serpent. Doesn't see too well. But then, neither do you."

"What do you mean?"

Hermes peered up at the gulls still screeching overhead. "Not driftwood, Sport."

VII
Sea Serpent

PERSEUS SPRANG TO HIS FEET and scanned the waves, holding out his hands to shade the nearly horizontal rays of the sun. The object, whatever it was, had been nearly half a league from shore, but he could no longer make it out among the indistinct shadows. He inspected the margin of water between, and that's when he spotted it.

It was a log, surely, most of it submerged, but with a thick, leafless branch still attached, bent over and bobbing many feet above the surface. Periodically the branch sank for several moments, only to rise again some distance closer, as if by the action of the waves. Perseus squinted, still unsure. Then he saw the humps.

There were three of them rising out of the water at regular intervals. The three became two, then one, and finally disappeared altogether as the tall form leading them slipped beneath the surface. Then they all rose at once, and repeated the process. This rhythmic undulation could no longer be taken for the random drifting of debris. Its steady progress toward shore was the conscious movement of a willful intelligence. When it was within a hundred yards, Perseus made out the earless, triangular head.

He'd heard stories of sea serpents all his life. They were supposed to be dragon-like, horned, with great scaly claws and flaring nostrils that breathed fire. But this creature, despite its huge bulk, had the form of a real snake. Though its cylindrical body was as thick as a tree trunk, it had the same black eyes, the same blunted nose, the same darting double tongue. Once on a winding mountain path on Seriphos, Perseus had been startled by a snake and nearly jumped out of his shoes. It was sunning itself on a rock—resting after a meal, apparently, for there was a grotesque bulge in its midsection where a luckless mouse, swallowed whole, was being digested. Perseus did not like snakes.

His first impulse was to flee, and who was better equipped? His winged sandals might take him several miles away in a matter of moments. Perhaps Hermes was right: he should mind his own business, continue on his way. His purpose, after all, was to save his mother, whose claim upon him was surely greater than that of Andromeda. The scornful princess neither asked his help nor seemed to appreciate it. Yes, why not flee? But then Perseus remembered the court, all the well-dressed nobility and their laughter at his expense. He remembered the smiling, condescending king and his raven-haired queen. How civilized the royal couple had seemed, how polished their speech. Yet they had shackled their daughter like an animal to be an animal's feast, to be the next hideous bulge in this serpent's gullet.

Perseus slipped off his cloak, bent his knees, and leapt into the air.

* * *

Andromeda was wrong about the length of the beast. Thirty feet was far too conservative. Hovering above the creature, Perseus put it at about twice that size. From this perspective he could see the banded pattern on its skin, black alternating with gold. Wet with sea spray, the colors shimmered in the late afternoon sun.

He circled overhead several times, staying out of the beast's field of vision and trying to formulate some plan of attack, but no strategy came to him. How does one fight a sea serpent? How does one kill it? In his whole life Perseus had never killed anything larger than a fish, and he didn't even do that particularly well. Dictys would inevitably shoo him away and do the job himself. Yet Perseus knew that whatever he did, he'd best do it quickly, for he was losing precious daylight. Able to come up with no better scheme, he determined to wait until the beast submerged and then surprise it upon surfacing.

Perseus swooped down, and as soon as the triangular head slipped beneath the waves, he positioned himself some distance in front of it. When he turned seaward again, he was blinded, staring straight into the sun. He shaded his eyes, tried to make out the form beneath the waves, but all he could see was the glare on the fluid surface. He hesitated, considered shifting his ground. Then all at once the sun disappeared. Rearing twenty feet in the air was the huge banded neck.

Paralyzed, Perseus watched the great jaws of the serpent fall open, revealing a pair of curved fangs, long as scimitars, and before he knew what was happening, these were flashing down through the air in his direction. Perseus dodged—not fast enough he feared—but unaccountably the jaws fell on empty ocean several yards from him, sending a salt spray high into the air and drenching his clothing.

Stunned as much by his escape as by the attack itself, Perseus hung there immobile, with rapt fascination as the huge head rose again in the air, its fangs dripping seawater. Reaching its full height, the serpent lunged once more, and Perseus leapt again. This time it struck even farther away from him, sending up another great splash. That's when Perseus realized it was the beast's poor vision causing it to strike at his elongated shadow, which danced madly about the waves.

There must be a way to exploit this advantage, he thought, but before he could come up with a plan, time suddenly ran out. The serpent whipped its tail in a broad arc over the surface of the water. With a slap, it caught Perseus behind the knees and knocked him into the sea.

Perseus flailed, gulping brine as he sank. Several seconds later, several fathoms down, he was finally able to get control of himself and remember his training. He was raised on an island and knew the dangers of panic in the water. Holding on to what little breath he had left, he stretched out his arms and slowed his progress downward, then looked for the glow of the surface.

The shimmering light was thirty or forty feet up, and he was just about to leap toward it when he saw the coiled shape spiraling toward him. Perseus was tempted to bolt, but was unsure if even his winged sandals could outdistance the beast through the water. Despite his terror and the pain in his lungs, Perseus stood absolutely still. Gliding back and forth the serpent wound its way downward until it was a mere dozen feet away, its black eyes looking directly into his. Yet it slid by unaware, its vision even worse underwater than in air. After an agonizing interval, Perseus watched the serpent swim away.

His lungs ready to burst, Perseus leapt toward the light and gasped for breath when he splashed to the surface. Then a strange thing happened. The fear that had so recently gripped him was now replaced by an unfamiliar emotion. As he had hung motionless in the depths, Perseus had not felt like a man, had not felt like a human being. For a brief, terrifying eternity, fathoms below the surface, Perseus had felt like prey, something to be impaled on a great curved tooth, to be swallowed, to pass through the guts of a snake. As he watched the serpent now, its undulating form moving so steadily, so rhythmically toward the beach, Perseus was no longer inclined to flee. He drew his sword.

When the beast submerged, Perseus counted the seconds it stayed under. When it submerged a second time, he counted again. When it submerged for the third time, Perseus inhaled deeply and slipped beneath the waves.

Although his winged sandals could not propel him quite so fast in the water as they could in air, Perseus was still fast enough to close with the serpent before it surfaced. Overtaking it, he dove under the creature. He paused long enough to grasp his sword in both hands and hold it at arm's length above him. Then he leapt upward. The serpent was just lifting its great head into the air when Perseus struck, driving the blade deep into the beast's neck.

In a paroxysm the serpent coiled itself around the epicenter of its pain and lashed the seas with its tail. Perseus pulled the sword free, dodging the twisting form, which rolled now in a rosy cloud billowing from its wound. He swam out of reach and emerged from the water some distance away. From here he watched the roiling maelstrom of bubbles and pale blood, waiting to see if the serpent would rise again in a final death throe. Instead, the turbulence subsided and the water became strangely calm. Then he felt a slight agitation beneath his feet.

Instinctively, Perseus shot into the air. Directly behind him was the gaping maw of the serpent. Rearing its head high above the waves, the beast snapped its jaws shut, inches below the winged sandals.

Perseus flew off, banked, then in a great arc homed on the serpent again. Blood still flowed from the gash in its neck, but the serpent lunged. One flashing fang caught the tunic leaving a jagged rent, but missing the skin. Perseus's sword was already in motion. He swung the bronze downward and struck the triangular head behind one of its dull black eyes.

For a moment the huge form hung in the air, as if suspended from above by an invisible cord. Then all at once it collapsed, falling to the waves with a deafening splash and sinking for the last time into the depths of the sea.

VIII
Bedfellows

TORCHES ALOFT, the night guards at the rear gate exchanged glances. Perseus, dripping brine and blood, announced to them that he'd just killed the sea serpent, and he demanded admittance to the palace. They were about to refuse when Andromeda appeared.

"Why did you come back?" she hissed as she pulled him into the walled garden, beyond earshot of the guards.

"Wasn't I supposed to come back after I killed the serpent?"

"*Did* you kill it?"

"Yes."

At the far end of the path she slumped onto a stone bench.

"What's the matter?" Perseus asked. "You don't seem very happy about it. They were going to feed you to that thing. Remember?"

"You shouldn't have come back."

"Why not? I had a bargain with your parents." Something occurred to him. "Wait a minute. I know what it is. You're afraid

I really intend to marry you. That's what you're thinking: that you, a princess, are going to be married to a peasant, and you'd rather be shackled to that rock again than be shackled to a poor slob like me."

"That's not it."

"Well, you can just put the thought out of your head. I only made that bargain to save you from marrying your damned toothless uncle. Once we get the hell out of here, we part company." He sneered. "It probably never occurred to you that a poor, dumb slob might not *want* to marry a princess."

She glared up at him.

"Surprised?" he asked.

"No. Only a *very* dumb slob *wouldn't* want to marry a princess."

Suddenly there was a commotion at the palace gates. Andromeda stood up as the king, the queen, and a small party of soldiers approached.

"We are told," King Cepheus intoned, eyeing Perseus, "that you claim to have killed the serpent."

"I *have* killed him."

"What proof did you bring?"

Confused, Perseus lifted the front of his tunic. "Proof? How do you think I got blood all over me?"

Cepheus flashed his mirthless, bland smile. "There was a braggart once who claimed to have killed a lion. He too was covered with blood, but it was the blood of a chicken."

The soldiers snickered.

"And did the lion return?" Perseus asked.

"You miss the sense of my homely parable. The point is—"

"The point is," Perseus interrupted, "if I didn't kill the serpent, then it should have returned today. Did it?"

"There have been no reports as yet, but one day does not provide sufficient proof that—"

"Well, how many days *will* provide sufficient proof? Two days? Three? I can wait. How many?"

No longer inclined to tolerance, the king glowered, but it was his wife who spoke next.

"Perseus," she said in deep, mellow tones, "do not think that we are not impressed, all of us, with the extent of your affection for our daughter. We have all felt the youthful passion in the blood that drives us to try any stratagem, risk any improbable falsehood in pursuit of love. Even as we admire the intensity of your ardor, we cannot let it blind us to the sober, religious duty of thanking our immortal benefactor. This very day we made a special sacrifice to the great God of the Sea, Poseidon, asking him to intercede for us and destroy the serpent."

Cepheus looked sideways at her but kept his peace.

"If, indeed," she continued, "the serpent does not return to Joppa in two, three, or even more days, we will know then that our deliverance is due, not to feeble human hands, but to the mighty will of divinity."

Queen Cassiopeia now trained her black eyes on her daughter. "And as for you, dear Andromeda, should this terrible doom truly be lifted from your head, we will with gladness take you to our bosom again and once more plan with joy the royal nuptials between you and your noble uncle."

Perseus grasped Andromeda's arm. Instantaneously, the soldiers leveled their spears.

"Let her go," the king said calmly.

"I'm taking her with me."

"No, you're taking her nowhere, and if you don't release her right now, you won't leave this garden alive. There's no way out of here for you, so just be a good boy and let her go."

Her smile dark, Cassiopeia soothed, "Please do not take too heavily, Perseus, your loss on the field of amour. You are young and will take up the gauntlet again. Accept your defeat with dignity.

It is the manly way. Now restore our dearest daughter to us." She reached out a jeweled hand.

His eyes on the spearheads, Perseus whispered to Andromeda, "Well? Do you want to stay or do you want to go?"

Andromeda met her mother's black eyes. "Go!"

"Hold on," he said, slipping his arm around her waist, and with that he leapt into the air.

Cepheus's mouth dropped open as he watched them ascend skyward. The queen cried to the dumbfounded soldiers, "Shoot him! Shoot him down with your arrows!"

The sergeant sputtered, "But ... but my lady, we might hit the princess."

"Damn you," Cassiopeia shrieked. "Shoot them down!"

As the two young people disappeared into the night sky, well out of bow shot range, they still heard the queen's howls far below. "Shoot them! Shoot them down! Shoot them *both* down!"

* * *

Andromeda drew up her knees and folded her arms around them as she gazed out at the moonlit sea. Behind her on the ridge Perseus rummaged in his leather bag.

"I don't have much food left," he said, "just some cheese. Do you want any?"

She shook her head.

"I thought I'd get some back at the palace before I left," he added. Perseus inspected the new rent in his soiled tunic. "I was kind of hoping to get a change of clothes too." He shrugged his shoulders, then sat by Andromeda's side and began to munch on the cheese. "Anything wrong?"

"No."

"Are you sure?"

"I'm sure."

"I thought you might be feeling bad or something."

"No. I feel great. Who wouldn't feel great after fleeing her home with only the clothes on her back, while her own mother is trying to have her killed?"

Perseus scratched his chin. "My mother always says she'd like to kill me too, but she doesn't really mean—"

"Why don't you just shut up," Andromeda snapped.

He frowned, took another bite.

After several minutes, Andromeda sighed deeply and looked over at Perseus. "So, what kind of cheese do you have?"

Wordlessly he broke the hunk in two halves and handed her one. Andromeda began to nibble. "What does your name mean?" she asked.

"My name?"

"I'm interested in names. What does 'Perseus' mean?"

"Killer."

"Really? Why did your father name you that?"

"It wasn't my father. It was my mother."

"Did your father die?"

"Not to my knowledge."

"Then why didn't your father name you?"

Perseus did not answer.

"Are you a bastard?" she asked.

"I think I liked it better when you were quiet."

She studied him for a moment. "Where are you really going, Perseus?"

"I told you already: Cimmeria. Where are *you* going to go?"

"Why are you going to Cimmeria?"

"None of your business."

"Is it a secret?"

"Yes, it's a secret."

"Tell me."

"No."

"Come on, tell me."

"If I do, will you tell me why you were so disappointed that I came back to the palace?"

"All right," she agreed. "It's a deal. Why are you going to Cimmeria?"

"To steal an old lady's eyeball."

Andromeda scrunched up her face. "Yuck."

"So why didn't you want me to come back?"

She stretched out her legs and looked toward the water again. "Because I knew my parents wouldn't keep their end of the bargain."

"Then why did your mother make such a big deal about insisting that I marry you?"

"My mother is sick."

"She looks healthy enough."

"Not that kind of sick. No offence, but she got a kick out of humiliating me by pretending she was going to marry me to you."

"Because I'm a nobody?"

"Yes, but don't feel bad. The marriage to rich Uncle Phineus was intended as a humiliation too. That was also her idea."

"I don't understand. Why should your own mother treat you like that?"

"My nurse told me once that the queen was envious of me."

"Why?"

"Strange as it may seem, for my beauty."

"*You?*"

"Astonishing, huh?"

"Well, no, it's not that. I mean, you're not bad looking. It's just that the queen is so ... glamorous."

Andromeda fell silent.

"So where are you going to go?" Perseus repeated.

"With you."

He shook his head vigorously. "No, you're not."

"Yes, I am."

"What makes you think so?"

"Well, realistically, Perseus, you can't leave me just anywhere. Without family or possessions, I'll either end up dead or a concubine. So I'll go with you. When you're done getting your disgusting eyeball, you can take me back to wherever it is you came from."

"Seriphos."

"Seriphos. And your mother can set me up at something."

"Like what?"

"I don't know. Whatever you common people do."

"You've got it all figured out. Well, I hate to disappoint you, but I'm not going home after I get the eyeball. I have to get something else first."

"What?"

"A head."

Again Andromeda grimaced. "Well, whenever you finish your revolting collection of body parts, you can take me to Seriphos."

Perseus swore under his breath.

"And as far as the sleeping arrangements are concerned," she continued.

"Don't worry about it."

"I don't intend to."

He sat silently for several minutes without looking at her. Then he grumbled, "What does *your* name mean?"

"Dominator of men."

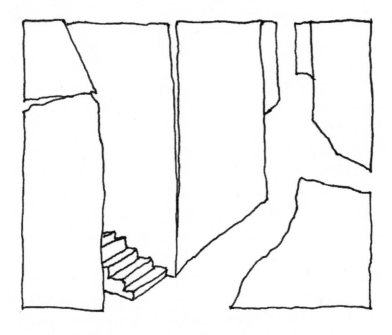

IX
Thief

TWO CANNOT FLY as easily as one. That became obvious as they headed south the next day. When Andromeda tried to hold on by locking her wrists around Perseus's chest, it put an intolerable strain on her arms, and the stranglehold constricted his breathing. For a while they avoided the obvious solution, but eventually squeamishness gave way to practicality. During a mid-morning stop Andromeda proposed that he carry her piggyback, with her legs wrapped around him instead of her arms. Consequently, when they were ready to go, Perseus presented his back to her, and Andromeda, hiking up her skirts, put one leg, then the other, around his waist, and hoisted herself up. Perseus, to support her, slipped his arms under her legs.

As she adjusted her position on him, Perseus noticed the softness and smoothness of her thighs resting on his forearms. He could feel her breasts too, slight bulges pressed up against his back. He felt an odd, troubling sensation.

For her part, Andromeda was coolly deliberate and pragmatic. When Perseus seemed to handle her legs too gingerly, she instructed him to lock his arms more firmly under them. In a businesslike manner she pressed her torso tightly against his back and draped her arms casually around his neck, her chin resting on his right shoulder. Content with her stability, she gave Perseus leave to take off. Once airborne, they immediately perceived the advantages of this new configuration, despite the bodily proximity it required. Perseus was able to steer more easily, and Andromeda could see better and thus help navigate.

The next consideration was food. Their provisions all but gone, Perseus set about getting more. By nightfall they had reached a small city along the Arabian Gulf, and thinking to replenish their supplies here, Perseus left Andromeda at a secluded spot along the shore and slipped into the quiet town alone.

It was not a Greek city; that was apparent. The buildings, the ships in the harbor, even the smell of the place seemed foreign. Careful to avoid evening strollers, Perseus passed through several twisting streets trying to figure out how he might obtain food. He had nothing to exchange; nor could he hope to earn it. Might he beg something from a kind stranger? But how, if he didn't even know the language?

As he ambled down one deserted alley, he chanced upon an open window with a large, round loaf of bread cooling on the sill. It seemed to glow in the moonlight, temptingly within his grasp. After darting his eyes in both directions, he slid silently along the wall and crouched beneath the window. Slowly he reached over his head. Instead of feeling the smooth crust, however, he felt another pair of hands just then lifting the bread from the sill.

A female voice screamed in terror. Startled out of his skin,

Perseus nearly screamed himself. As the loaf fell to the ground with a crunching thud, Perseus raced down the alley and ducked into an adjacent street. From here he ran down another block, then another, until the scream had long since died away. He hunched over to catch his breath.

"You know, Sport, for a guy who can slay a sea serpent, you sure make a lousy thief."

Perseus looked up and glimpsed Hermes leaning against a darkened house across the street. Sullenly he replied, "I don't like being a thief."

"Why not? It's a noble calling. I ought to know. I'm the patron god of thieves. Besides, some people have way too much as it is, don't you think?"

"That doesn't mean it's right to steal."

With a sly smile Hermes crossed over to him. "You didn't seem to mind stealing a certain princess."

"That was different."

Perseus peered down the street, seeing if there might be another opportunity to snatch something. Hermes followed his gaze.

"Forget it, Sport. You're no good at this. Give us your satchel there."

Perseus hesitated, then untied the leather bag from his belt and handed it over.

"Observe a professional." Coolly, Hermes crossed back to the house he had been leaning against, stopped at the window long enough to wink at Perseus, then scrambled silently over the sill and disappeared.

Minutes passed. Alone outside and nervous lest an alarm be raised, Perseus continually looked about him, expecting at any moment to see a chance citizen walk by. More time passed, and he could not imagine what was taking Hermes so long. Finally a figure appeared in the darkened window. First one leg draped over the sill, then another. His arms encumbered, Hermes hopped down silently and with a satisfied grin sauntered back across the street. "Child's play," he announced.

Suddenly there was shouting from within the house, and a large man leaned out the window yelling incoherently and waving a great curved sword.

"Come on," Hermes shouted. "Let's beat it!"

Again Perseus found himself running through the deserted streets, Hermes by his side. When they had left the neighborhood far behind, they both came to a stop.

"Child's play, huh?" Perseus gasped, leaning over once more and panting heavily.

"Hey, the guy's a light sleeper," Hermes shrugged.

"Who was he anyway?"

"Oh, don't worry about him. He's loaded, sells camels for a living. Greedy son of a bitch would sell his own sister if she wasn't homely as sin."

"What took you so long anyway?"

"I got you some things. Here," he said, handing over the bulging leather bag. "I relieved the camel dealer of some of his gold—it's under the food—so next time you can buy your own."

Perseus frowned but tied the bag to his belt.

"And here, take this. You look a disgrace." It was a neatly folded tunic. Last of all Hermes draped a blanket over his arm. "This'll keep you warm on cold nights."

"Only one?"

"How many blankets do you need? You're going to the tropics, for God's sake."

"Well, there are two of us."

"So? You can both fit under it."

Perseus shifted uneasily.

"Oh, for crying out loud." Hermes put his hands on his hips. "I forgot. Middle class morality rears its ugly head! Well, I'm sorry, Sport. I'm not going back into that maniac's house just to get you a

second blanket. You two children can just sort it out between you."
He paused. "Now, do you remember the directions?"

"Yes."

"The three rivers and everything?"

"Yes."

"Good, because I'm going to be busy for a while and may not be able to keep an eye on you."

"I'll be all right."

Hermes turned to leave, then stopped and looked again at Perseus. "By the way, you did pretty good back there with the serpent. I was impressed."

"Thanks."

"Dumb, though, not to slice off the nose or the tail or something so you'd have proof that you'd killed it. You're just not getting the hang of being an epic hero."

* * *

When Andromeda awoke the next morning, she found herself covered by a warm blanket. Sleepily she sat up and examined it. The pattern was unfamiliar and the weave different from that practiced in her own country. She looked up at Perseus, who was already awake and seated nearby. No longer dressed in his tattered clothing, he wore a fine new garment of rich, dark blue material.

"Where did you get these things?" she asked.

"In town," he answered absently. "You want something to eat?"

"You stole them."

"I suppose so."

"Who did you steal them from?"

"A camel dealer."

"Did you kill him?"

"I had to. He drew a sword on me."

"You're a *barbarian!* "

Perseus took two small rounds of bread from the bag and

tossed one onto the blanket. Her hunger at war with her scruples, Andromeda hesitated.

"You might as well eat it," Perseus told her. "He's dead anyway."

She sighed, picked it up.

"Be careful, though. He bled on some of the loaves."

She dropped it as if it were on fire. When she looked at Perseus again, he was smirking. "Liar! You didn't kill anyone."

While she ate, Andromeda ran her hand over the smooth fabric of the blanket, which Perseus had obviously placed upon her as she slept. She glanced over at him. "That's a nice tunic."

"Do you think so?"

"Of course, it's not your size," she added, "and the color is putrid." After a while and in a softer voice she asked, "Why are you really going to Cimmeria?"

"I told you."

"Yes, I know. You told me what you're supposed to get there and what you're supposed to get afterward, but you haven't told me *why* you're doing these things."

"Do you really want to know?"

"Yes."

He told her. He told her about his mother and King Polydectes, and about his mission to slay the Gorgon. He told her about the appearance of Hermes, the divine gifts. He told her the whole story, and he told it matter-of-factly, as if it were the account of any mundane experience and not a recitation of marvels. When he was done, he swallowed the last of his bread.

Andromeda stared at him for several moments, then murmured, "I wish you couldn't fly."

"Why?"

"Because then I wouldn't have to believe a word you said."

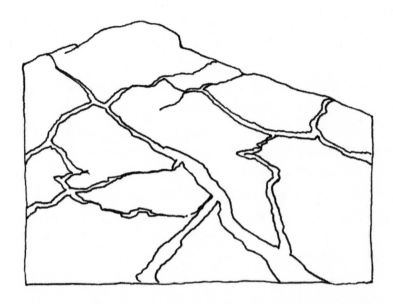

X
Cimmeria

THE FARTHER SOUTH they headed along the coast of Africa, the fewer signs of human settlement they saw, just impenetrable jungle, vast plains filled with herds of curious beasts, and endless miles of barren coastline. On the fifth day Perseus was lost in thought all morning as they flew. Though he could feel Andromeda pressed against his back, her chin resting casually on his shoulder, he had come to take for granted this odd, limited intimacy between them. Suddenly, though, he was roused from his reverie when she asked, "What did Hermes look like?"

"I don't know. He looked like anybody else."

"Well, was he tall, short, young, old?"

"He seemed about my age. He wasn't particularly tall."

"Was he good looking?"

"I guess."

"The gods are supposed to be beautiful." She was thoughtful for a moment. "Did he have an extraordinarily long penis?"

"For God's sake, Andromeda!"

"Well, in the statues he always has an extraordinarily long—"

"He was *dressed*, for the love of Zeus!"

"Oh." She fell silent, looking down at the seacoast far below them, a white ribbon of beach caught between the blue ocean on the one side and the shady depths of green foliage on the other. After a while, and in as nonchalant a tone as she could summon, Andromeda asked, "How many women have you slept with?"

He looked askance at her, their cheeks only inches apart. "That's none of your business."

"I was just curious."

Perseus sneered. "Curious about how dissolute we common folk are—right?—compared to you aristocrats. How would you like it if I asked you how many men you've slept with?"

"I'd tell you."

His brow furrowed uneasily. "How many?"

She nodded her head several times, as if counting to herself. "Five."

His eyes opened wide. "Five?!"

"No, wait. Six."

"*Six!*" Perseus turned away. Setting his jaw, he said stonily, "So what? I don't care."

"Why should you care?"

"I *don't* care."

"Good."

They both were quiet for a spell. Then Andromeda laughed. "Don't be so gullible, Perseus. I was just kidding. Of course I've never slept with anyone. What kind of a marriage could my father have made for me if I had? I only said that because of your crack about aristocrats. Why do you harp so much about being common?"

"Because I *am* common."

"Well, everybody's got faults. That doesn't mean you have to broadcast them to the world." She shifted her weight slightly and tightened her legs around him. "So will you tell me now?"

"Tell you what?"

"What I asked you—how many women you've slept with."

There was a note of defiance in his voice. "None."

"Really? Weren't there any young women on Seriphos? You know, milk maids, that sort of thing?"

"Of course there were young women."

"You haven't been injured, have you?"

"No."

Andromeda pondered for a moment. "You're not one of those Greeks who likes boys, are you?"

"No."

"Well, I wouldn't mind if you were. I mean, everyone's entitled to their own preference, no matter how disgusting it is."

"*I don't like boys!*" he shouted.

"All right, all right. I'm right here." She paused. "So then how come you've never slept with a woman?"

Perseus rolled his eyes. "Because I don't believe in doing that with just anybody who comes along. And furthermore, I don't see why I should have to explain myself to—"

Something on the horizon caught his attention. Andromeda followed his gaze to a second land mass lying several leagues offshore from the coast. Too large for an island, it seemed at first the pointed headland of a vast neighbor continent. But when Perseus veered seaward to find its eastern coastline, he discerned the unmistakable oblong shape Hermes had drawn in the sand.

"Cimmeria."

* * *

They skirted the eastern seaboard and soon recognized the three-hundred-mile reef. Harder to discern were the three rivers that emptied into the sea from obscure mouths behind the reef. Perseus covered the entire length of the island to make sure he'd located all three, then doubled back to follow the middle one from the coast.

The country rose quickly once they headed inland, and Perseus found that he and Andromeda were carried upward nearly as much by the rising currents of air as by the winged sandals. Below him the river meandered calmly through a thin forest, but up ahead he could see the torrent from which the placid stream emerged. A sheer cliff five hundred feet high marked the boundary between the lowlands and the upland region, and over this cliff the river fell, sending up a perpetual cloud of white vapor. In the opposite direction of its flow, they swept over the waterfall. Once above the ridge, Perseus stopped in midair.

It was an unearthly landscape that greeted them, part primeval jungle, part smoking, barren wasteland. A crooked line of volcanoes marched along the central axis of the plateau and looked for all the world like the bony spine of the island, broken and festering with rage. Some sent thin ribbons of gray steam high into the upper atmosphere. Others belched thick, dark billows that hung threateningly close to the earth. Around them in a broad swath several miles wide was a sea of black rock that had choked all the vegetation.

"My God!" Andromeda gasped. "It does look like the edge of the world."

Perseus was able to follow the river from above for a while, as it wound through the jungle foliage. After a time, though, the river diminished to a smaller and smaller stream and began to disappear beneath the thick green canopy. At that point Perseus descended to the jungle floor.

"What exactly are we looking for?" Andromeda asked as she slipped down from his back.

"An abode where the sun never shines."

"Poetic, Perseus, but not very specific."

The jungle was hot. It also buzzed with insects that stung and harried the couple mercilessly as they pushed through the dense undergrowth. Mud spattered their legs and their clothes as they slogged along beside the stream. For a while Andromeda lifted her skirts and tried to pick her way carefully, but in time she gave up the effort as hopeless.

They followed the stream for two hours until, much diminished, it flowed down the center of a wide rocky bed. Perseus feared it might dry up entirely before they found its source. Meanwhile, the trees became sparser, the undergrowth thinned, and jagged, pockmarked black stones were scattered more and more abundantly on the soft earth. Finally when Perseus pushed aside a stand of ferns, he found himself at the edge of the vast field of rubble that led to the row of smoking peaks. He paused for a moment to marvel at the desolation, then wordlessly ventured out onto the barren waste. Andromeda followed.

Despite the broken ground, the going was easier here, and fewer insects plagued them, but the heat was oppressive. Without the green canopy, they had no shelter from the unforgiving sun. Noting the intense glare Andromeda remarked that this was a very unlikely locale for a place where the sun never shined.

The stream seemed to originate somewhere out in the lava flow, and when the ground began to rise toward an extinct hollow peak, Perseus wondered if the source would be the volcano itself. As he rounded a curve on the steep path, though, he found his answer. The water, no more than a rivulet now, flowed steadily from a black hole in the side of the mountain.

XI
Gray Women

"WHAT DO YOU MEAN, 'wait here'?" Andromeda protested.

"Just what I said." Perseus was on his knees peering into the opening, which was hardly a foot high and little more than two feet across. The bright sun and an overhanging ledge prevented him from seeing anything inside but blackness. The floor of the cave, though, was lined with stones, smooth from the steady stream of water that flowed over them.

"If I stay out here in this heat, I'm going to be fried by the time you come back."

Perseus squinted up at the sun and saw the truth in Andromeda's argument. "Well, then, go back and wait in the jungle."

"And get eaten alive? No way. I'm coming inside with you."

He sighed resignedly. "All right, but don't go any farther than the entrance."

Perseus fell to his stomach, then slithered over the wet stones into the hole, pulling his shoulders through first, then his torso. Finally, Andromeda saw his legs and feet disappear into the darkness.

"Perseus?" she called after him. "How is it in there? What do you see? Perseus?" She crouched down and peered into the darkness. "Perseus?"

Suddenly his hand shot out into the sunlight, startling her. "Come on, if you're coming."

She cast a momentary glance at her already soiled clothing, then lay down on the wet stones as Perseus had done. Grasping his hand, she pulled herself through the hole.

Andromeda could see nothing at all inside, and though she could feel the hand gripping hers, she could not see the person attached to it.

"The ceiling's high enough to sit down in here," Perseus told her. "Reach over your head and touch it."

She felt the moist rock a full arm's length above her. Andromeda pulled herself into a sitting position, her wet garments clinging to her now, and she felt chilled.

"If you turn around," Perseus said, "you can see the light at the entrance where you came in."

She looked back. The wet stones glistened in the mouth of the cave.

"As long as you stay within sight of that," he cautioned her, "you can get out by yourself—just in case anything happens."

"In case anything happens? What do you mean? We *flew* to this godforsaken place. Remember? How am I supposed to leave without you?"

"Good point. So nothing better happen. Just stay put."

"How are you going to find your way if you can't see anything?"

"It seems to be a tunnel. I'll feel my way."

"You might get lost."

"I can't get lost," he said as he crept away from her. "I'm under the protection of the Olympian Gods."

"But I'm not," Andromeda muttered to herself. After listening to the shuffling, scraping sounds recede into the distance, she took one last look at the shimmering stones at the cave mouth, then got on her knees and began to crawl.

* * *

The walls were damp to her touch. Andromeda slid along the right side, but stretched out her hand to the left to make sure that the tunnel did not diverge somewhere along its length. Even on the darkest night back in Joppa, when not a star shone through the little window in her room, Andromeda had never experienced a gloom so utter, so palpable as this. Her vision gone, her starved senses took in every damp stone, every rustle of her chiton along the floor. At first she crept hesitantly, fearing to overtake Perseus, but after hearing no sound of him for some time, she feared never catching up at all and quickened her pace.

As she moved through this appalling blackness, Andromeda thought of her old nurse. Whenever she was frightened as a little girl, her nurse would sing a silly song about a duck named Penelope. Unconsciously Andromeda hummed the tune now, taking some comfort from the sound of her own voice.

Her sense of time seemed to have gone dormant with all her other senses, and she had no idea how long she'd crawled. Suddenly, though, she stopped and froze against the wall. In the darkness up ahead were voices. Indistinct, muffled, and distorted, they might have been mistaken for the chirping of birds. Andromeda proceeded slowly, and she began to see flickering reflections that became brighter as she pressed forward. Then up ahead where the tunnel took an abrupt turn, the walls blazed from some source unseen. Now she could distinguish the individual speakers. There were two of them: creaking voices, old voices, women's voices.

"You know what I really think—" one said.

"Yes, I know what you really think," the other interrupted.

"No, you don't. You don't know what I *really* think."

"I certainly do know what you really think."

"All right, what do I think?" the first one asked.

"I'm not going to say," the other replied. "Because if I say what you really think, you'll say you don't think that."

"Because I don't!"

"Yes, you do."

"No, I don't."

Andromeda flattened herself on the tunnel floor and slithered the last few feet, then peeked around the corner.

Two old women, one exceedingly fat, the other very thin, were seated on the ground in the center of a large, open cavern. Dressed in dusty, shapeless black garments, their long gray locks falling nearly to the floor, they were both bending over a small pot on the fire. Though Andromeda couldn't see their faces distinctly, something in them appeared bird-like. Puffy pink jowls hung below the fat woman's cheeks. Taut, nearly transparent skin stretched over the thin woman's bony features. Despite their differences, they appeared to be sisters, for they each had the same down-turned, sharp nose like a parrot's beak.

"I like good, hot soup," the thin woman announced.

"You like it *too* hot," said the fat woman, stirring the pot.

"I don't like it *too* hot. It's just that *you* don't like it hot *enough*."

"I don't like it so hot that it burns your mouth."

"No, you like it cool so you can eat it fast," the thin woman rejoined, "and then you get the collywobbles."

"I don't get the collywobbles from eating fast."

"Yes you do. You complain about the collywobbles every day after dinner. Do you ever see me get the collywobbles? I don't, because I eat slowly."

"You never get the collywobbles because you never make the dinner," the fat woman countered.

"Do you want me to make the dinner? If you want me to make the dinner, all you have to do is tell me."

"I didn't say that I wanted you to make the dinner. I'm just saying that I get the collywobbles because I always have to worry about making the dinner *just so* for you."

"You don't have to make the dinner just so for me. All I said was that I like my soup to be good and hot."

"You like it *too* hot."

At that moment Andromeda was startled by a shadow moving along the cavern wall. In the dancing firelight Perseus was crawling slowly along the ground and making his way behind the two figures.

The fat woman stopped stirring. "I think it's done."

"Is steam rising from it?" the thin woman asked.

"Yes, a little steam."

"How much steam?"

"I don't know how much steam. *Some* steam."

"Well, is it just one sickly little stream of steam, or is it a good, healthy swirl of steam?"

"Oh, here," the other said disgustedly, "look for yourself!"

The fat woman lifted her face into the firelight now and plucked a single eyeball from one of the two hollow sockets in her forehead. Andromeda gasped aloud.

"*What was that?*" shouted the thin woman as she reached for the eye. She was an instant too late, however. Springing from the gloom, Perseus snatched the eye from the fat woman's hand.

There was a horrifying screech, as from a swooping eagle. The thin woman leapt up, her eye sockets as blank as her sister's, and she exposed a row of jagged, pointed teeth. She spread her cloaked arms like two black wings and flew toward the sound—flew directly at Andromeda.

Andromeda scrambled to her feet, forgetting the low ceiling, and she knocked her skull against the rock. The last thing she saw before she passed out was a crazy vision of her old nurse, eyeless, singing, and bearing the feathered countenance of a duck.

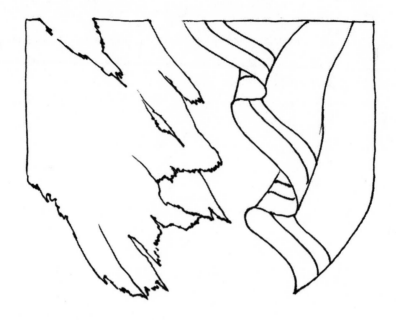

XII
Divestment

"ANDROMEDA? ANDROMEDA?"

She felt Perseus shaking her but saw nothing in the blackness. "Where are you?" she cried, grabbing at him. "I can't see. Am I blind? Did they take my eyes?"

"You're lucky they didn't. Why the hell didn't you listen to me and stay put? You damn near got us killed back there." He relaxed his grip. "Don't worry. We're still in the cave. That's why you can't see anything. How do you feel?"

There was an aching throb in her head. Andromeda reached up and gingerly fingered the bump. "Ouch!"

"I had all I could do to keep those two harpies off you. I think they would have eaten you for dinner if they could have agreed on the recipe. Luckily, I had the eyeball, and they were willing to negotiate. Can you crawl? I was able to carry you this far, but the tunnel gets narrower here."

"I think so." Andromeda felt for the ceiling, then rose to her knees and followed Perseus back through the passage. Soon she saw the glimmering of wet stones at the entrance. Outside again in the dazzling brightness, she shaded her eyes and stumbled away from the cave, then plopped down on the rubble. After a while she said quietly, "Listen, I want to thank you. I mean, for getting me out of there."

Perseus did not respond.

"You have every reason to be sore," she went on. "I could have botched things up for you. I should have stayed by the entrance. Anyway, I just wanted to tell you … I'm sorry."

Still Perseus was silent.

"Well, why don't you say something, for heaven's sake? What do I have to do, get on my knees?" Andromeda turned around only to discover that Perseus was gone.

With difficulty she raised herself to her feet again and scanned the barren lava field. Not only was he nowhere to be seen, but there was nowhere for him to hide. She returned to the mouth of the cave and peered inside. "Perseus? Are you in there? Perseus?" There was no reply.

She straightened up again, baffled, but trying not to panic. That's when she spotted him, less than ten feet away and standing where no one had been a moment before. He was in the process of removing a cap from his head.

"I guess it works," Perseus remarked. "You didn't see me at all, did you? Clothes or anything. It's a Cap of Invisibility. This is what I stole the eyeball for—to trade it for this. Hermes says it'll allow me to approach the Gorgons. Here, you want to try it?" He handed it to her.

Woven of fine gray wool, the cap was dome shaped, with a thick red band around the edge to hold it tightly on the head.

"It was the strangest feeling," Perseus continued. "I could

see everything: you, the cave, the volcanoes. But something was different. It took me a while to figure it out, and then I realized: it was my nose. I wasn't seeing my nose anymore. I guess you're not usually conscious of seeing your nose, but when it's suddenly invisible, you'd be surprised what a difference it makes. Don't you want to try it?"

She shook her head and returned the cap to him. "It looks better on you."

* * *

They made camp in a cluster of palm trees near the shore, not far from the river they had followed inland. While Perseus laid out the blanket, Andromeda strolled down to the river's edge. She frowned at her soiled clothing, remembering her handmaidens in Joppa who used to do her laundry for her.

"I'm going to wash my chiton," she called over her shoulder. "Myself too," she added, noting her spattered legs. "Do you want me to wash your tunic for you?"

"Sure," Perseus answered absently.

She ambled back and waited expectantly. "Well?"

He looked at her. "Well, what?"

"Your tunic. Can I have it? How else can I wash it?"

"Oh." He shifted uneasily.

"What's wrong? You've already seen *me*. What's the difference? If we're going to be together for God knows how long, I'm not going to go without washing my clothes, and I hope *you* don't plan to. Here, I'll take off mine first, if that makes it easier for you." She began to unfasten the two brooches on her shoulders, but when Perseus averted his eyes, she stopped. "Oh, all right," she sighed disgustedly. "You can go in the bushes over there and toss it out to me."

Perseus glanced at the bushes but made no move toward them. He stared for a long moment at Andromeda's nearly black eyes, which were staring sternly back at him. Wordlessly, he drew his bronze sword and stuck it into the ground, then loosened his belt. In one motion he pulled the tunic over his head.

Andromeda hesitated, trying to ignore the unaccountable thumping in her chest. Raising her chin slightly, she unfastened the brooches, untied the cord, then coolly let the gown fall and stepped out of it. She held out her hand toward him. When Perseus did nothing but stand there, confused, she jabbed her finger at the tunic. He delivered it over.

Turning on her heel, she strode back toward the water. "I suggest you wash yourself too," she said. "You're a sight."

* * *

They left the island behind the next morning and traveled north, retracing their route along the coast of Africa. As they flew, Perseus puzzled over the previous evening. After Andromeda had washed their garments and spread them out on a large rock to dry, she'd unbraided her hair and returned to the water to bathe herself. Perseus joined her, and when they had both scrubbed off the mud and grime, they'd sat together on the bank while their clothes dried.

Perseus could not help snatching a glance or two at his companion. Though he had seen her nude before, of course, he was surprised to find that he was looking at her differently. He was struck by the smoothness of her skin, the delicacy of her features, the appealing litheness of her slender body. As she leaned back on her hands, her dark brown hair, which had always been tied up in two long side braids, fell thick and luxurious behind her as it dried in the late afternoon sun.

But what Perseus found even more surprising was the naturalness of the experience. He would have expected their nudity to dominate his consciousness while he reclined with her on the bank, but in fact, as they chatted away idly about inconsequential things, swapping stories about their homelands, he eventually forgot that they were naked and was only reminded of it when their clothes had dried and they dressed again. Now, flying along with her clinging to his back as usual, her chin resting gently on his shoulder, they both were acting as if nothing had happened. And of course, nothing *had* happened really, and that in itself seemed the most baffling thing of all.

Suddenly his thoughts were interrupted by Andromeda's voice very close to his ear. "Where are we going next?"

"I'm not sure. Hermes was kind of vague in his directions. I've got to stop soon, though, to get some more food."

"You mean steal some more."

"No, I can buy it this time. I have gold."

"Which you stole," Andromeda added, but she said it with a smile. "So where will you stop?"

He shrugged his shoulders. "I wish we could find a place where we wouldn't stick out like a sore thumb."

"Let's go to Egypt," Andromeda proposed.

"Egypt? Why?"

"The biggest cities in the world are in Egypt. Ships from all over stop there. They're used to foreigners."

"Have you been to Egypt?"

"No."

"Then how do you know so much about it?"

"Come on, Perseus. Everyone knows about Egypt. Haven't you ever heard of the pyramids?"

XIII
Owl

PERSEUS HAD HEARD of the pyramids, but had never expected to see them in his lifetime. Nor had Andromeda, for that matter, but three days later, the great pointed shapes loomed on the horizon.

On the north coast they located a sprawling port city, its harbor filled with merchant ships of every description. Perseus alighted in a vacant alley, and from here the two walked the rest of the way to the populous market area, bustling with humanity. Perseus had never seen so many people all in one place, in such a variety of costumes, and speaking such a multiplicity of languages. At wooden stalls piled high with goods, buyers and sellers haggled at the top of their lungs.

Jostled along in the crowd, Perseus would have pressed on quickly to fill his bag with food, but Andromeda lingered over the jewelry on display, the exotic clothing, the rich carpets. Finally Perseus split his gold with her and arranged to meet her back at the alley in an hour's time. Then he proceeded on his own.

Finding food was no problem, for food was to be had everywhere, and in the greatest abundance and variety. Braised meats, fish, and sausages filled the air with tempting aromas, but Perseus was looking for more homely fare that would not spoil so quickly. Eventually he bought some flat loaves of bread, a hard block of cheese, and some dried figs. Unused to bargaining, and not understanding what anyone said to him, Perseus knew that he probably overpaid, but he filled full his leather bag. Just as he was about to return to Andromeda, he spotted a stall hung with skins of wine. He hesitated, gazed at them longingly.

The vendor was a small, round man, and as soon as he noticed Perseus, he beckoned him closer and pressed one of the skins into his hands. Perseus squeezed it, felt the liquid slosh inside, could almost taste its sweetness. The vendor rattled in an incomprehensible tongue, urging him to do something. When Perseus looked blankly back at him, the round man reached over and pulled the stopper from the neck, then thrust the skin under his nose. The aroma was heady, exhilarating. Without further ado, Perseus reached into the leather bag for more of his gold.

The wineskin slung around his neck, Perseus turned to leave when he was arrested by the sight of a woman close to him. Dressed in a fine Greek chiton, she was perhaps thirty years of age or perhaps older … or was it younger? Her features were not so much lovely as they were perfect. Her gray eyes, straight nose, thin lips, high forehead, even her hair, which was pinned in majestic swirls upon her head, were absolutely regular, completely symmetrical. More striking than her flawless appearance was the look of placid serenity on her face, a countenance more fitting a statue than a human being. She was leaning over the stall, surveying the wares, but the vendor paid no attention to her. Then suddenly she spoke.

"The skins of goats."

Her voice was deep, resonant, drowning out all the cacophony of the marketplace.

"Are you talking to me?" Perseus asked.

"Goats," she repeated, straightening up now. She was tall for a woman, taller even than Perseus himself. "They are penned and milked while they are young, eaten when they become too old to bear, and finally skinned after they are dead, so that their hides can be filled with fermented fruit. Humans are like gods to the goats, are they not?" She flashed her gray eyes at him. They were calm, tranquil, despite the hubbub all around her.

"I … I don't understand."

A half-smile played briefly on the woman's lips. "Come with me," she said.

Perseus hesitated, but she was already striding away from him. He glanced over his shoulder, then surprised himself by scurrying after her.

She moved briskly, the throngs parting almost automatically as she passed. Several times Perseus feared he would loose her in the crowd, but finally caught up when she joined a small cluster of people at the stall of an armorer. Stacked upon the table, hung by leather straps from the scaffolding, scattered indiscriminately on the ground was a vast collection of bronze implements of war: swords, spears, shields, helmets, daggers. Presiding here was a large, powerfully built man, shirtless and bald.

"Reach me that helmet over there," the woman directed.

Perseus looked at her. "What would you want with a helmet?"

"The one with the azure plume," she added.

Puzzled but unable to resist, Perseus lifted the helmet from the stall and passed it to her. She examined it carefully, turning it over in her hands. She felt the thickness of the metal, ran her fingertip across the eye slits, then shocked Perseus by slipping it on her head. He expected to hear ridicule from the onlookers, but no one seemed to notice. Meanwhile, the woman shook her head slightly inside the helmet, testing the fit, the visibility, the degree of protection. Perseus marveled at how natural she looked in it.

"Not bad," she commented approvingly as she slipped it off and glanced over at the proprietor. "Yonder muscular fellow is no Hephaestus, but he's not bad."

Perseus quickly laid the helmet back on the stall. "How do you know so much about armor?"

"It's my business to know." Her attention was now drawn to a collection of shields displayed on the ground. Tooled upon the bronze were images of gods. Perseus recognized Poseidon raising his trident, Apollo strumming upon his lyre, Zeus enthroned in glory and wielding a thunderbolt. But there were other deities he'd never seen before, monstrous, composite beings with the bodies of men and the heads of birds or jackals. He found the inhuman shapes strangely troubling.

"Pay them no heed," the woman advised, following his gaze. "They never existed, nor ever shall. They're merely the unruly imaginings of a barbarous nation. They need not concern you."

She pointed to a small, unadorned round shield set to the back of the others, put aside, perhaps, until the armorer found time to decorate it. "Fetch that one."

Perseus lifted the shield from the ground.

Its curved polished surface reflected her own image back at her as the woman inspected it. She slipped her left forearm through the leather strap at the back and hefted it, bearing it before her body, feeling its weight and balance. Again, her ease and dexterity astonished Perseus. She handed it back to him. "Buy it."

"Buy it? I haven't got enough gold for something like this."

She flashed her gray eyes. "The skilled gentleman over there will make one bad bargain today and sell it to you for what you have. Buy it," she repeated.

Defying her was futile. The shield in one hand, the remainder of his gold in the other, Perseus approached the armorer, who was haggling with another patron, but broke off when he saw the blond-haired young man. He eyed the shield, then the gold. Perseus expected him to protest that the payment was too little for so fine a product of his art. Instead, he made a brief nod to show that the deal had been struck, then scooped up the pittance of gold and turned back to his other customer.

When Perseus returned with the shield, the strange woman was already threading her way through the crowd. He took off after her, leaving the marketplace and bearing toward the harbor. She glided past the busy docks, past the loading and unloading ships, and finally paused at the far end of a deserted wharf.

Perseus came to a stop, panting. "Don't you want your shield?"

She observed it placidly. "One day, but for now it's yours. You'll need it to slay Medusa."

"How do you know—"

"Must I carry an owl around so you'll recognize me?"

He staggered backward. "Oh my God! Athena!"

"You're not very clever." Glancing at his calves she added, "Not very sturdy either, but you were chosen."

"I'm sorry. I didn't expect … I never thought—"

"No, not so clever by half as Odysseus. He would have known me right off."

"Who's Odysseus?"

She turned from him, gazed out at the water. "My favorite of your kind. He's not born yet, but in all the seasons of your race, from its insignificant beginning to its melancholy end, there will be only one like him. He'll be the wiliest, the shrewdest, the most cunning—the best liar too."

"You admire those things?"

"Of course I do."

"But you're the Goddess of Wisdom. You can't consider those things virtues."

The half smile flitted across her thin lips. "You Greeks have a wonderful way of using words. It shows your own wiliness, in spite of your moral pretensions. Goddess of Wisdom indeed! You must know, Perseus, that I'm the Goddess of War. Why else would your own artists always picture me in arms? And if I personify intelligence, it's the guile, subtlety, and deceit that win battles. It's your own guilt about those qualities that induces you to gloss them over by calling them wisdom. Your very emblem for me gives you away. What is an owl but a creature of stealth, who hunts by night on silent wings, mercilessly ripping out the throat of its prey?"

Perseus shook his head, bewildered. "I always admired you. Even when I had doubts about the other gods, I thought you were different, special."

"I am special. Your countrymen will create the most enlightened city on earth, and it will be named after me. At the highest point in that city they'll construct the most graceful temple ever built, and dedicate it in my honor. None of the gods, not even Zeus my father, will be revered so much as I am."

"But it'll all be a sham. We might as well worship one of those beast gods with the head of crow."

Anger flashed across Athena's countenance, but just as quickly the accustomed look of tranquility returned. "You have spirit, despite your spindly legs, but don't let it run away with you."

Perseus stood silent for a moment, then held out the shield. "What am I supposed to do with this?"

"You're to use it as a mirror. Since you can't look directly at the Gorgons, you'll look instead at their reflection in this shield."

"Is there anything else?"

"Yes. I want you to go to the city of Deicterion on the island of Samos before you attempt to slay Medusa. Painted on the wall in my temple there you'll find an image of the three Gorgons. Medusa is the one in the center. I want you to study that image carefully so that you don't slay the wrong sister. Do you understand?"

"I understand," he said, an unmistakable resentment in his voice.

"What's the matter, Perseus?"

"You use us. You're using me right now to take revenge. That's all you gods do is use us, but you don't really care about us. It doesn't matter how much we pray to you, or sacrifice to you, or build you temples. You treat us as if we're nothing."

The half-smile returned again. She slipped around behind him and leaned to his ear. "If the goats prayed to you, if they burned incense in your honor, would you stop milking them? Would you stop slaughtering them? Would you stop rendering their precious skin into a lifeless vessel, serviceable merely for conveying wine?"

Perseus spun around to reply, but he was alone now on the empty wharf.

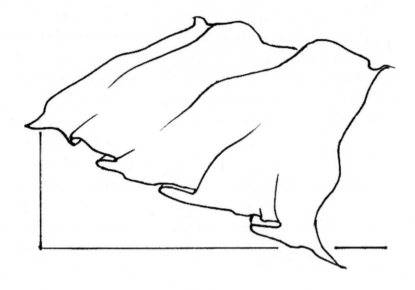

XIV
Rites of Bacchus

ANDROMEDA HAD PREVAILED upon Perseus to make camp near the pyramids, and she couldn't settle down to dinner before approaching one of the great tombs and actually laying her hands upon it. The rough surface was warm to the touch, still throwing off heat absorbed from the sun all day. Andromeda's eyes traveled up the sharp edge to the pinnacle far above. The dark silhouette blotted out a vast triangular portion of the heavens.

Meanwhile, Perseus had plopped down on the blanket some distance away and was absently picking at one of the loaves. She glanced over her shoulder at him. He had been late getting back to the alley, and when he did return, he seemed gloomy and dejected. She'd asked him how he came by the shield slung over his back, but his mumbled response did little to enlighten her.

Andromeda ambled to the blanket now and sat by his side. After fishing some of the dried figs out of the leather bag, she looked toward the pyramid again.

"Who do think is buried there?" she asked after a moment.

"A king, I guess."

"I wonder if his queen is buried in there with him," she mused.

Perseus lifted his shoulders, not really paying attention.

"I think it would be lonely to be out here all by yourself, don't you?"

He did not respond.

Andromeda noticed the wineskin where Perseus had dropped it on the blanket. "Hey, what have you got there?" She reached over for it and pulled the stopper. "Wine! You got us wine! They never gave me wine back at the palace. Only a ceremonial little sip on special occasions—like my mother's birthday. Of course *she* drank all she wanted." Andromeda held out the skin to Perseus. "Would you like some?"

"Go ahead."

She hesitated, then lifted the skin in the air and squeezed some of its contents into her upturned lips. She shuddered at the first swallow. "Got a bit of a bite to it, Perseus. I hope you didn't pay too much for it." She eyed the skin dubiously, but lifted it to her lips again. "Well, it's not *too* awful." She held it out to him.

Perseus took a long draft, then wiped his lips with the back of his hand. "We've got to go to Samos."

"What for?"

"To see a picture of the Gorgons."

"Why do you need to see a picture?" she asked, lifting the skin again.

"So I don't chop off the wrong head."

Andromeda swallowed hard. "You know, Perseus, I can't make you out sometimes. Just when I think maybe you're not so bad—"

"I know."

They continued to pass the skin back and forth, and soon Perseus began to feel the soothing effects of the wine. The cool night breezes, refreshing after the heat of the day, began to waft away his gloom. Andromeda, unused to spirits, was falling even more easily under its sway. She leaned back. "It really is wonderful being here, isn't it? Seeing things we've never seen before, and being so free. I had no freedom as a princess. Someone was always watching me. Did you feel free back in Seriphos?"

"I never thought much about it."

"I had no fun either," Andromeda continued. "I know that probably sounds strange to you, but it's true. You probably enjoyed life more than I did, despite your straitened circumstances. I bet you had fun just going out fishing with ...." She paused, furrowing her brow. "What was his name, again?"

"Whose name?" Perseus asked, raising the wineskin.

"You know, that quaint old peasant you told me about. Oh, wait, I remember. His name was Dryope, right?"

Wine sprayed out of Perseus's mouth as he burst into laughter. "Not Dryope! Dryope means woodpecker!"

Andromeda laughed now too, covering her face with her hands and leaning over into his lap. Perseus put his arm around her, and for a while they shook giddily in unison, their silliness out of all proportion to the error that had provoked it. Repeatedly each of them, sensing a breach in decorum perhaps, tried to settle down, but then one or the other would think "woodpecker" again, and they would dissolve once more into a chorus of giggles.

Several minutes and several false starts later, the humorous fit finally spent itself. Breathing deeply, Andromeda straightened up, and Perseus removed his arm. Glancing at each other, they smiled bashfully.

"I almost forgot!" Andromeda exclaimed, leaping to her feet. "Wait here."

She plucked something from the blanket and then disappeared in the shadow of the pyramid. When she emerged a few minutes later, she was no longer wearing her traditional chiton, but a much more exotic gown, silky, close fitting, her left shoulder bare.

"What do you think?" She made two or three half-turns in front of him. "It's Egyptian."

"It's ... very beautiful."

Andromeda seemed enormously pleased with this response and settled next to him again, several inches closer this time. Almost without thinking, Perseus slipped his arm around her waist, and she leaned against him affectionately. Together they viewed the unworldly scene spread out before them. Andromeda gazed up at the star-filled heavens.

"How high can you go, Perseus?"

"Not as high as that," he said, looking upward also.

"It's such fun to fly. I'd rather fly than be a princess." She snuggled closer to him. "I'd rather fly with you."

Perseus squeezed her. He then found himself stroking her side, her bare shoulder, feeling the warmth of her skin beneath his hand. Then she tilted her head up and looked at him. There was no hostility in her face any longer, no disdain, but a new and unusual seriousness Perseus had not seen before. She closed her eyes, and with this invitation Perseus bent and kissed her.

Andromeda's lips were soft and her breath intoxicatingly sweet. He kissed her again, then again. He put both arms around her and pulled her to him tightly, feeling her slight figure, so appealing in the silky gown. He had been blind not to notice before how lovely she was. Perseus kissed her again more slowly and more deeply, and he thrilled at the touch of her fingers on his neck. They fell backward on the blanket, suddenly gripping each other with a strange, frightening necessity.

Perseus ran his hands over her body with a familiarity that fairly shocked him, and she offered no resistance. Dimly he was aware that their judgment was muddled by the wine. To take advantage of her in this state would be wrong, and he knew it. He should stop right now, take the time to think about what he was doing, not give way to passion like a creature without scruples. But as he felt the allure of her slender body pressed against him and inhaled the natural perfume of her skin, Perseus did not stop.

When he reached up to remove the single brooch that fastened her gown, Andromeda moaned. Perseus fumbled with the clasp, the trick of its simple locking mechanism escaping him. Frustrated, he was tempted to rip it from the gown. He sat up to get a better look at it. The small ivory disk glowed in the moonlight.

"What's the matter?" Andromeda asked softly. "I can open it for you." She began to undo the clasp, but was arrested by the queer expression on his face. "I bought it in the market where I got the gown," she explained. "Is there something wrong with it?"

Perseus let go of her and moved away.

"What's the matter?" she repeated. Andromeda looked down at the brooch now herself and the figure represented there. "It's Egyptian, but it symbolized one of our goddesses too, so I thought it might bring us good luck—you know, since it's an owl."

* * *

They barely spoke to each other the next morning. Their things packed up, Perseus wordlessly presented his back to Andromeda, and she climbed upon him in silence. It was only after they had been airborne for nearly an hour that Perseus summoned the courage to speak. He took a deep breath. "I want to apologize for what happened last night."

"Nothing happened," she snapped.

"I know, but I wanted to say—"

"I don't want to talk about it."

"Well, I just wanted to—"

"I said I don't want to *talk* about it."

Perseus fell silent.

After a few moments Andromeda muttered, "I don't know how I could have been such a fool—to have stooped so low."

"You have every right to be angry," he said.

"Angry? I'm not angry. I'm disgusted. I'm disgusted with myself. I'm revolted with myself."

"It was all my fault," he assured her. "I'm sorry—"

"*You're* sorry? I'm the one who should be sorry! To think what I almost did—and with you, a nobody, a peasant, a common rustic, for God's sake, a bumpkin!"

Perseus heaved a sigh and determined that it would be better under the circumstances to say no more on the subject. He was grateful at least that there wasn't something worse to regret. With this small comfort Perseus retreated into his own thoughts.

Moments later, however, Andromeda howled in his ear, "How could you! How *could* you! How could you *turn me down?*"

XV
Apparitions

THE ISLAND OF SAMOS lay just off the coast of Asia Minor, but when Perseus caught sight of it several days later, he was thinking about a different island, Seriphos, barely a hundred miles to the west. He pictured his mother in the little house they shared, wondered what she was doing at this hour. Though he'd been away only a matter of weeks, it seemed much longer. He bit his lip, gazed down at the odd, bird-shaped island coming into view.

Andromeda peered over his shoulder, her voice close to his ear. "Is that Samos?"

He nodded.

Though there was a lingering embarrassment over the night in Egypt, Perseus and Andromeda had resumed their normal routine together. If they were slightly more reserved now, Perseus didn't mind. He was thinking more and more about the task ahead of him, and he didn't want to infect Andromeda with his anxiety.

Two mountain peaks dominated the interior of Samos, and the city of Deicterion was perched halfway up one of them, all its low dwellings clustered around an elevated citadel. Perseus alighted in a wooded area outside of town where Andromeda would be safe. Leaving his leather bag and his weapons in her charge, he entered the city alone.

Deicterion was a far cry from the bustling port in Egypt. Its sleepy, slow-paced rhythms reminded Perseus of his own island home. The humble buildings were familiar, as were the clothes the people wore, but what Perseus appreciated most was to hear his native tongue again. Two men carrying great jars of oil argued in Greek. A woman shouted to her neighbor in Greek. A knot of children shrieked to each other in Greek.

Though Perseus had been able to locate the citadel easily enough from the air, he found that negotiating a path to it on the ground was another matter. The city was an exasperating maze of winding narrow streets. Several times he thought he was heading toward the center of town, only to end up in the suburbs instead.

His frustration mounted as he quickened his pace, but each lane that he entered seemed to lead him farther afield or back around to where he had been before. Though he could have asked directions, to do so would mean revealing he was a stranger, and he didn't want to be asked difficult questions.

Down one particularly dusty thoroughfare, Perseus became conscious of footsteps behind him. He had passed many people as he strode along, but these steps seemed more determined somehow, as if they were bent on overtaking him. He ducked into a side lane, and when the other made the same turn, he hastened forward, walking so rapidly now that the only way to go any faster was to break into a run, something he dared not do. Yet the footsteps seemed to be gaining on him. He was just about to stop altogether and meet his pursuer face-to-face when a voice called out: "Hey, slow down, Sport. I can't keep up with you."

Perseus whirled around.

"You're moving awful fast for a guy going in the wrong direction. The temple's back that way," Hermes said, jerking his thumb over his shoulder.

"I was wondering when you'd turn up again."

"Like a bad penny, right? Come on, I'll walk you."

Together they proceeded back the way they had come.

"I've been watching you," Hermes said. "You've done pretty well. Your chroniclers will be pleased. You got the cap from the old biddies, and now you've got the shield. Hey, what did you think of Athena? Real sourpuss, right?"

Perseus did not respond.

"Don't worry. She has that effect on everybody. No sense of humor—you know what I mean? Now, using the shield as a mirror? That was her idea; I'll grant her that. You want anything sneaky, that's right up her alley. But I told her I could get the shield for you as well as anybody. She didn't have to come herself. But no way José! She wasn't going to trust anybody else to pick it out. Fancies herself an expert, you understand. If you ask me, she takes her job too seriously. People like that spoil it for the rest of us."

At the next intersection, Hermes paused, scratched his head. "This way," he concluded, pointing left. Before they had gone more than a few steps, he stopped, looked over his shoulder. "No, come to think of it, it's that way."

They did an about-face.

"But enough shop talk," Hermes continued. "I've got to tell you how to get to the Land of the Hyperboreans. That is, if you're still game for tackling the Gorgons."

Glumly he responded, "I'm still game."

"Good. Now it's an island again, but north this time, northwest actually." Hermes gave him the directions, and to make sure the young man got them correctly, he had Perseus repeat them back to him. By this time they had reached the temple, a small, columned building, its dark interior not visible from without.

"Well, this is where I leave you, Sport."

"You're not coming inside?"

"No, thanks. I've seen the picture before. But you take a good long gander because if you peek once at the real thing, you're in deep weeds, Sport. Boulder city. Rock of ages. You'll be your own tombstone, if you take my meaning."

Perseus scowled.

"What's the matter, Sport? You got a bug up your address?"

"Back on Seriphos you told me I was under the protection of the Olympian Gods."

"So you are."

"Then why do you keep warning me that I can get killed?"

"Because you can."

"Well, what kind of protection is that?"

Hermes folded his arms. "You know, Sport, the problem with your species is that you invent your own gods, endow them with all the qualities and capabilities you think they ought to have. Then when one of us actually comes down here to lend a hand, you're disappointed because we don't fit your image. Hell, of course I can't protect you if you screw up and look at one of those snake-haired bitches. Besides, if I *could* protect you, that wouldn't make you much of a hero, would it?"

"I don't feel like much of a hero anyway." Perseus climbed the steps of the temple and slumped against one of the columns.

"Buck up, Sport. I got faith in you." Hermes followed him up to the landing and put his arm around his shoulder. Immediately Perseus felt the familiar tingle course through his body. "Remember, it's not the size of the dog in the fight; it's the size of the fight in the dog." He gave him a squeeze, then dropped his arm. "Now, you've got the directions?"

"Yes."

"Good. And don't lose that blanket. It's chilly where you're going. The Hyperboreans like it well enough, but I'll take your climate down here any day. To each his own, though, right? Live and let live." Hermes shuffled down the steps.

"Will the Hyperboreans tell me how to find the Gorgons?"

"Oh, you'll have no trouble finding the Gorgons," Hermes called back. "Hell, they're surrounded by stones."

* * *

Seated on a fallen log by the edge of the woods, Andromeda played idly with Perseus's sword, using its point to doodle on the ground. For some reason she was thinking of the old seer back in Joppa. She'd visited him shortly after the king and queen announced her upcoming marriage to Uncle Phineus. The kindly old man had ushered her into his little cottage, served her a bowl of soup while he performed the augury, then told her what the future had in store. She was destined to marry a relation of hers and give birth to five children, all boys. Andromeda put a small purse into the old man's hands, but she felt no joy in the prophecy, which only sealed her fate. In the days that followed, she tried to take some comfort in the five sons promised her, for she liked children, but she found it impossible to separate them from the hateful marriage that would produce them. When the sea serpent plagued the city and she was selected to be its victim, she had almost welcomed it as her only escape. Then out of nowhere Perseus appeared. What did it mean? Could the old seer have been mistaken?

Andromeda looked up toward the mountain path and spotted Perseus returning. On impulse she slipped her arm into the shield strap and lifted the sword to greet him in a mock battle stance, but when he was close enough for her to see the dazed expression on his face, she abandoned the jest and quickly put the weapons down.

"Are you all right?" she asked.

Perseus hesitated, as if to concentrate on the words spoken to him. "Yes. Sure."

"Did you see the picture?"

He nodded absently.

"Well, what did they look like?"

"Who?"

"The Gorgons."

At the word, Perseus started with such queer ferocity that Andromeda unconsciously backed away from him. He recovered quickly and flopped down on the log. After a moment Andromeda sat down beside him.

"Perseus, what happened?"

"Nothing. Nothing, really. I'm just a little preoccupied, that's all." He forced a weak smile. "I've been thinking, though. We're not far from Seriphos. Maybe it would be a good idea if we went there first. Then you could stay with my mother—until I get back, I mean."

Andromeda stared at him. "You don't think you're *coming* back."

"Of course I'm coming back, but there's really no reason for you to go along. Remember what you said down in Cimmeria about being stuck there if something happened? Well, since we're so close to home now, there's no need for you to take that risk again. You could just—"

"I'm going with you."

"Don't be silly. I won't be away all that long. Besides, you'll like my mother. At least I think you'll like her. In any case, you'll be safe there, and then—"

"I'm going with you," she repeated.

All pretence dropped from his features. "You can't."

"I can, and I will."

"Andromeda," he said softly, "you don't know what I saw."

"I don't care what you saw," she announced with finality. "I'm going with you."

"But why?"

"Because I gave up five sons for you."

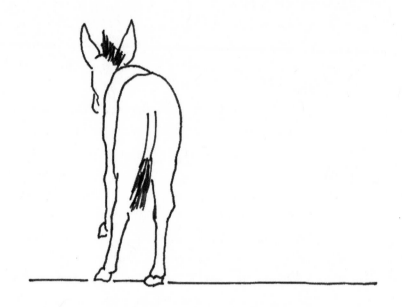

XVI
Land of the Hyperboreans

THERE WERE GREAT RIVERS below them, winding through a green countryside. They skirted jagged white peaks that formed a barrier to all but flying creatures like themselves. But they saw no cities, no settlements. Though it was summer, the climate was cooler as they traveled north, and gray clouds often blotted the sun. When it rained, which it did frequently, these were not the warm showers that would be welcomed back home, but biting storms, blown by an unforgiving northwest wind. During the day the couple wrapped the blanket around themselves as they flew, and at night they huddled together beneath its warmth.

It was Andromeda who suggested it the first cold night, when their only shelter was an overhanging rock ledge. Perseus joined her under the blanket, and for a while they lay several inches apart, careful not to touch one another, but as they began to doze, their bodies, instinctively seeking warmth, rolled next to each other. When he awoke the next morning, Perseus found his arm wrapped around Andromeda, and her head nestled cozily on his chest.

* * *

"You'll know you've reached the right island," Hermes had advised him, "when you see the cliffs. They're a hundred feet high, and white as death."

Passing over the narrow channel that separated the isle from the mainland, Perseus saw them now, sheer and pale, rising out of a sea of fog.

Andromeda shivered slightly. "Who would want to live way up here?"

They swung around to the southern shore where they located a smaller island that shielded a cove. As they headed inland, they scanned the countryside looking for signs of human habitation, but long before they saw a single dwelling, they heard the music.

There were lyres, flutes, and drums, and as they came within sight of the village, they heard voices singing. The tune might have been unfamiliar to Perseus, but the music was not. Thousands of miles from his native land, Perseus recognized the unmistakable strains of Greek song.

On the far side of a small hill outside of town, Perseus concealed the sword and shield under some brush. Then they proceeded on a rutted path toward the village. Before they had gone a hundred steps, they were hailed from behind.

"Where's your ass?"

Laboring up the hill was a stocky, sixtyish man leading a donkey. His dress, like his tongue, was Greek. When he reached them, the stranger steadied himself from the exertion by laying his hand heavily on Perseus's shoulder, nearly knocking him off balance.

"I swear to Zeus the Jester," he panted, stooping over, "this hill gets higher every year." He took a deep breath, then patted Perseus's shoulder by way of thanks before removing his hand. "Where's your ass?" he repeated. "You're going to the Copulation, aren't you?"

Perseus stood silent in his bafflement.

"Don't tell me you—." The stranger stopped short, noticing Andromeda as if for the first time. He looked her up and down, regarding her figure beneath the thin gown. "Oh, excuse me. You're a *dancer*!" He stretched out this last word with appreciative awe.

Andromeda smiled bashfully. "I'm not a dancer."

"You're not?"

She shook her head, reached over to pet the donkey's nose.

"Oh, but you must be," the stranger insisted. "You have the figure of a dancer, the lithe form, the slender torso, the long legs, the sensuous thighs—"

"She's not a dancer," Perseus snapped.

Immediately the man straightened up, assuming a sober, apologetic demeanor. "I beg your pardon, Sir," he said in a very correct voice.

Under Andromeda's glare, Perseus softened his voice and explained, "Where I come from, only whores are dancers."

"I understand completely," the man assured him. "You must forgive me. I had no idea." After a moment he asked, "And what are whores?"

"You don't know what whores are?"

"No, but please tell me so that I can avoid them."

Confused, Perseus looked to Andromeda, who merely grinned, enjoying his predicament. "Well, whores are ..."

"Yes?" The man was all attention, as if eager to commit vital new information to memory.

"It doesn't matter."

The man nodded, raised his hand. "Say no more. Every country has that which is ungraspable, untranslatable, concepts a foreigner can never understand. We Hyperboreans probably have some of our own. Suffice it to say that these whores, whatever they are, must be a plague to you, and there's an end. Where are you from, Sir?"

Perseus hesitated. "Seriphos."

The man pursed his lips. "I can't say I've heard of it, but take no offence at that. I'm no good at geography. Seriphos is a fine name, though. It sounds like a fine place. But it's overrun by whores, is it?"

Andromeda giggled, and the man seemed charmed by her merriment.

"It's not overrun by whores," Perseus muttered.

"Well, that's a relief." The stranger was serious again. "You must tell me, though, young man, how you learned to speak Greek so well. I could only tell you were foreign by the slight twang in your voice. A trifling mispronunciation here and there is the only thing that gives you away. You must have practiced a great deal to be able to speak now with so small an accent."

"I don't speak with any accent at all," Perseus countered irritably. "*You* speak with the accent. I'm *from* Greece."

The stranger stared at him for a moment, a look of delighted surprise overspreading his features. "You're from the Motherland?" He threw his arms around the startled young man. "Oh, my boy," he exclaimed, "*we're* from the Motherland!"

"You come from Greece?"

"Yes. Our ancestors did, at any rate." He pulled back and held Perseus at arm's length, the better to look at him. "This is wonderful! You're the first one from the Motherland ever to visit us. My name is Eumelus. You must come down to the village with me. Everyone will want to meet you. And this evening nothing would please me more than if you and the young lady would honor me by staying in my home and joining me and my family for dinner."

Before Perseus could demur, Andromeda answered, "We'd love to."

Eumelus yanked the rope to rouse his donkey. Then he stepped between the two young people, and, grasping their elbows, hurried them along the path. "Now, you must introduce yourselves on the way, and don't be shy. This is just wonderful, splendid! And to think you arrived at such an auspicious time too: right in the middle of our festival of Apollo the Lover!"

* * *

The event Eumelus had been hastening toward was just beginning as they arrived. A noisy crowd that might have comprised most of the village was gathered around a fenced pasture where scores of donkeys, male and female, had been set loose. Eumelus shouldered his way up to the fence where merry citizens were laughing and hooting, encouraging the beasts to do what they seemed quite eager to do anyway. The Copulation, Eumelus explained, was a rite honoring the Hyperboreans' patron god, Apollo, who took special joy, it was said, in watching lustful asses cavorting in pleasure.

Perseus had grown up around livestock, and was familiar enough with the coupling of animals, but a display such as this—dozens of beasts mounting each other to the gleeful clamor of spectators—embarrassed him. Several times he tried to coax Andromeda away, but she, for whom such a sight was not a commonplace, seemed rapt. The festivities lasted for about an hour; then, weary perhaps, or bored, the citizens began to disperse. As Eumelus led the couple through the village, he introduced them to friends he met along the way, and everyone seemed as delighted to meet them as he had been.

Eumelus's home was a modest dwelling of two stories, which housed three generations of his large family, all of whom appeared at the door when they arrived. Pulled inside, Perseus and Andromeda were hugged, patted, their arms pumped mercilessly, and they were buffeted with questions from young and old. What was the Motherland like? How long had it taken them to get here? Were they hungry? This last query seemed the most pressing of all. Before they could even answer, they were ushered to places of honor at the dinner table.

For weeks Perseus and Andromeda had survived on meager fare, bought or stolen from whatever source. They were not prepared for what was to follow. Dishes began to arrive, and soon the board sagged under the load: broiled fowl, roasted pork and lamb, grilled fish laden with butter, steaming vegetables in pungent sauces, cheese of various kinds, pitchers overflowing with wine, and baskets piled high with warm bread.

Eumelus noticed Perseus's astonishment and explained that this lavish banquet was part of the festival rites. Something in Eumelus's manner, though, made Perseus suspect that normal workaday fare was only slightly less grand. In any case, famished as they were, Perseus and Andromeda did not scruple. They devoured the feast, as their delighted host pressed fresh dishes upon them.

Over dinner Eumelus told his guests the story of the Hyperboreans. Their ancestors had been refugees from a war in the Motherland, what war he had no idea, for he was not good at history either, but they had sailed as far as they could from the fighting. When they came ashore here, they liked what they saw and settled down. How long ago this was he could not say, but many generations.

"Do you have a king?" Perseus asked.

Eumelus shook his head. "We've never felt the need to form a government."

"What about an army?"

"We have no enemies."

"But you must have laws."

"No. We rely on good manners and the arts."

"The arts?"

Hyperboreans, Eumelus explained, prided themselves on their appreciation of the arts. He rhapsodized about painting, about sculpture, about music. He described the two types of poetry, the heroic verse that the ancestors brought with them from the Motherland and the new verse that had developed here. The former was serious, stately, elevated in language, ennobling in character. The more recent was youthful, innovative, ironic, realistic. But to the Hyperboreans, the crown of all the arts was dance. After apologizing once more for his mistake about Andromeda, Eumelus explained the naturalness of his error. Dancers, male and female, are the most respected artists, and though anyone might aspire to become a dancer, only a very few have the natural bodily configuration.

Though Eumelus had been quite lucid in his explanation of all the other art forms, he failed utterly when it came to dance. He used metaphors that were not apt, superlatives that fell flat. He resorted to mystical terms, but lapsed into such impenetrable blather that he himself recognized his inadequacy. Finally he admitted that he could no more explain dance to them than one could explain love to someone who has never been in love. Perseus and Andromeda would simply have to attend the Muse's Dream that evening and see for themselves.

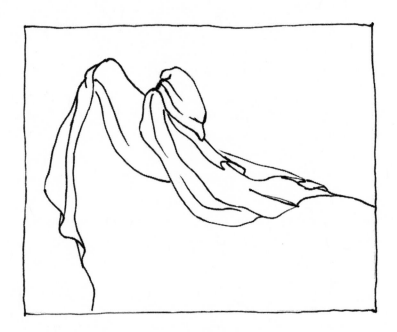

XVII
Muse's Dream

"LEGEND HAS IT," Eumelus told them as they threaded through the darkened street, "that the Muse Terpsichore herself came here long ago to teach us the art of dance. The Muse's Dream commemorates the event. It's the high point of every festival."

"Listen," Perseus whispered to Andromeda, "if this drags on too long, I'll make up some excuse so we can leave."

"You know, Perseus," Andromeda hissed back, "you are a first-class boor. Did it ever occur to you that some people might enjoy it—might even get something out of it?"

Dozens of torches illuminated a circular, grassy plot, around which a multitude of people were seated on the ground. It looked at first as if Eumelus and his guests would have to sit quite far back, but as word rippled through the assembly that the visitors from the

Motherland were there, a passage opened up, and room was made for all three at the very front.

Cross-legged on the damp grass, Perseus sighed impatiently, anxious for the dance to begin, anxious for it to end. He glanced around at the crowd. This happy-go-lucky people, who loved the arts and who needed no magistrates to rule them, no soldiers to protect them—what did they know of the Gorgons? The island was large. The monsters could be hundreds of miles away. Yet they could be over the next hill, and this heedless company would be none the wiser. The hideous image of Medusa from the wall painting on Samos rose up before his eyes, and Perseus shivered visibly.

For a while there was murmured conversation, an occasional laugh, a greeting to latecomers while the mellifluous sound of flutes and lyres drifted on the soft summer breeze. Then, with no apparent signal, talking ceased and a dreamy quiet descended. The musicians, after a momentary pause, took up a different strain. Preoccupied as he was, Perseus hardly noticed the shift, the excited expectation in the air. What finally intruded on his consciousness was the strange, haunting tune that filled the night with melancholy. Then, suddenly, the dancers appeared.

Ghostlike they floated into the magic circle, nine women, appearing all but naked in their thin, gauzy gowns. Golden laurel crowned their heads, and their hair fell free. With mesmerizing fluidity they whirled, spun, and swayed in the firelight, electrifying the air and barely touching the ground.

Fretful as he had been but a few moments before, Perseus now sat transfixed, conscious only of the ethereal creatures that glided before him. He looked from one to another, enthralled by their subtle, supple undulation, their gossamer beauty, yet it was an unfathomable something in their eyes that most confounded him. They betrayed neither joy nor sorrow, but a rare blitheness. Even while they vaunted the sweetness of life, they whispered of mortality. They danced, as one must always dance, on the edge of the grave.

* * *

Perseus and Andromeda were quiet on the way back to Eumelus's home. Their host showed them to a small room provided with two comfortable pallets pushed cozily together. After bidding them goodnight, he discreetly closed the door behind him. Though neither of them had slept indoors or on a real bed in a long time, they both appeared embarrassed by the too snug accommodations. Sleeping next to each other out in the elements had the rough endorsement of necessity, but this was different. Perseus chose one of the pallets, then casually, as if merely to adjust it, he shoved it a few inches away from the other. Without a word, they retired to their separate beds and both slept rather poorly.

In the morning Eumelus offered them horses so that they could view the countryside. Andromeda quickly accepted, but Perseus, seeing an opportunity to speak to Eumelus alone, decided to stay behind. He was pacing the floor when Eumelus returned from the stable.

"Your young lady must really be an experienced rider," Eumelus commented. "She picked the best mare of the lot, and when I told her—"

"Can we go for a walk?" Perseus was agitated, couldn't wait.

"I'd love a walk."

They headed out toward the hill where Perseus and Andromeda had first arrived, and for a while as they strolled, Eumelus plied his guest with questions about the Motherland. He was visibly dismayed, though, by what he learned. Greek history seemed but an endless catalog of wars, political struggles, intrigue, and the most atrocious villainy. The old poetry spoke of such things, but Eumelus thought affairs of that kind were all in the distant past. He was disappointed to learn that they still occurred with alarming regularity. Eventually he wanted to hear no more about the Motherland. There seemed a subtle change in his attitude toward Perseus too. Though Eumelus was as courteous as ever to his guest, he no longer exhibited the same degree of deference or awe.

When they reached the hill and began to climb it, Perseus finally broached the subject that was foremost on his mind.

"Eumelus, have you ever heard of the Gorgons?"

The older man looked thoughtful. "The Gorgons," he repeated, as if trying to remember something. "Oh, you mean the Lovely Ones."

"The Lovely Ones?"

"Yes, that's what we call them. I haven't heard the other name since I was a boy. I'd almost forgotten it."

"What do you know about them, the Lovely Ones?"

"Oh, it's a delightful story. Parents often recite it to their children, especially little girls who don't think they're very pretty. There were three sisters, plain women all, but the Splashing God Poseidon became enamored with one of them. Megera was her name, and after he made love to her, all three sisters were miraculously transformed into beautiful goddesses with the most luxuriant tresses. Is that the version you've heard?"

"Close enough. Do you believe the story?"

Eumelus eyed him curiously. "Do I believe it?"

"Yes, do you believe in the Lovely Ones?"

"What an interesting question! I didn't take you for a philosopher, Perseus."

"I'm not a philosopher. I just want to know if you believe in them."

"Forgive me," Eumelus said, "but the very nature of your query is philosophical. We often discuss such questions here, usually over wine by the fire, and we find the speculation fun."

"Well, I'm not asking this for fun. I need an answer. Do you believe the Lovely Ones exist?"

Eumelus stopped to rest now and catch his breath. "You don't like poetry, do you, Perseus?"

"What does that have to do with it?"

"Nothing really, except that it makes it very difficult for me to answer your questions. When you ask me if I believe the Lovely Ones exist, I remember a time when I heard a bard sing about them thirty years ago. My wife and I—she wasn't even my wife then—were sitting under a tree on a warm summer's evening, and we listened as the old man chanted and strummed his lyre. The bard's dead now—been dead, oh, longer than you've been alive, I'd say. So I guess *he* doesn't exist anymore, but the Lovely Ones still do, in that song of his. You see what I mean? It's a philosophical question."

"In other words, you don't really believe in them," Perseus concluded.

Eumelus shook his head. "My boy, my boy, you miss the whole point. I believe in them as much as I believe in Zeus, as much as I believe in our special patron Apollo, as much as I believe in any of the gods or any of the marvelous stories."

Perseus stared at him. "Wait a minute. Are you telling me that you don't think the gods exist either?"

"I'm telling you no such thing."

"You *are*. That *is* what you're telling me. You're saying that the gods only exist in poetry."

"My quibble with your interpretation is the word 'only.' You don't acknowledge the significance of poetry." Eumelus studied his younger companion. "Let me ask you something, Perseus. Is a poem a lie?"

"If it's about something that's not factual, it's a lie."

"But the facts don't always fit the verse."

Perseus scowled.

"I'm sorry," Eumelus chuckled. "I'm being facetious, and you want me to be serious. All right. Would it bother you if we didn't believe in the gods?"

"No, it's not that. I didn't believe in them myself until—well, it doesn't matter. But I don't get it. You told me about all your festivals, celebrating everything from Hephaestus's limp to the pimple on Poseidon's ass, for all I know. If you don't believe in the gods, why the hell do you make such a fuss over them?"

"Do you see something wrong with celebrating?"

"Yes, if the thing you celebrate is a fiction."

Eumelus resumed climbing. After a few moments he asked, "Did you enjoy the dance last night?"

Perseus hesitated. "Yes."

"I'm glad. I thought you would. Your young lady appeared to enjoy it too. She is a delightful young woman. You're very lucky. No offence, but she would have made a fine dancer. I want to ask you something, though, about what you saw last night. We love that dance here. Heaven knows, we love all dance, but that particular one especially. We look forward to it at every festival. It's in honor of the Muse Terpsichore, as I told you, and I suppose by your definition, we Hyperboreans don't really believe in Terpsichore. So I put it to you, Perseus: do you think we should stop holding the Muse's Dream since the Muse doesn't exist?"

Perseus wanted to say yes. He almost did say yes, but then the ethereal women in their gauzy gowns floated through his mind, swaying to the haunting music. "No, of course you shouldn't stop holding it, but why can't you just call it something else?"

"Ah, but the name is part of the thing, Perseus, and that's where the poetry comes in. Would the Muse's Dream still be what it is? Would the dancers still dance their hearts out the way they do? Would we in the audience still get that chill up our spines, exciting, exhilarating, and terrifying all at the same time? In short, would any of that godlike magic take place at all if we had to start calling this precious treasure of ours the Civic Holiday Frolic?"

Perseus heaved a sigh. "Can you just answer one question for me?"

"Certainly."

"The story you know—about the Lovely Ones—where was it

supposed to take place?"

"Right here on this island."

"And where did the Lovely Ones take up residence after their ... transformation?"

"So the story goes, not far from here. It's a quaint old structure."

"You've *been* there?"

"Yes, many times."

"And nothing happened?"

Eumelus smiled quizzically. "My word, what was supposed to happen?"

"And others have gone there too?"

"Of course. It's especially popular with lovers, for obvious reasons."

"It must not be the place. It must be somewhere else. Either that or you're right, right about the gods, right about everything, and I'm completely wrong. Maybe I've been dreaming all this time." Perseus glanced down at his winged sandals. "But I wasn't dreaming."

He had come to a stop now, for they had reached the place where his equipment was hidden. With his foot he pushed aside the brush, revealing the sword and shield.

"My God!" Eumelus exclaimed. "Weapons? You brought weapons here? Who in the name of Zeus did you intend to fight, my boy? Us?" When Eumelus saw the confusion and dejection in his downcast face, he suddenly felt sorry for the younger man. "What is it, my boy? Why are you so interested in the Lovely Ones anyway? Listen, maybe you'd like to see the spot for yourself. It might do you good. You could ride there tomorrow. Andromeda can take you."

His head snapped up. "Andromeda?"

"Yes. I told her about it this morning. She seemed quite taken with the idea of going there, especially when I mentioned the stones."

"*Stones!*"

"Yes, they're quite peculiar, actually, and some folks think—"

"Where is it?" Perseus demanded.

"Where's what?"

"This place, where is it? I've got to go there *now*."

"But, my boy, surely you can wait until—"

"*Where is it?*"

Astonished by his passion, Eumelus pointed. "North."

Perseus slipped the shield over his shoulder, then lifted the sword.

"My boy, what's the matter? You don't need those things here. There's no one who'll harm you." Eumelus grasped his arm. "Is this all you Greeks know? Swords? Blood? Death?"

"How many of the lovers who went to this place never returned?"

Taken aback by the question, Eumelus seemed confused. "Some. They eloped, that's all, and ran away."

Perseus pulled his arm free and shoved the sword into his belt. Grimly he regarded the older man. "You think just because you don't believe in a lion, it can't rip your throat out." He stepped away now, looking north.

"It's miles from here," Eumelus warned him. "At least come back to the house first so you can get a horse."

"I don't need a horse."

With that, Perseus crouched slightly, then leapt into the air.

XVIII
Circle

To be out on her own like this! Alone, riding, no one watching her—it was like the rare mornings in Joppa when she'd rise before dawn, silently lead Nutty from the stable to slip out of the palace grounds before anyone awoke. Of course, invariably her old nurse would be standing in the doorway as she tiptoed by. Then would come the litany of admonitions and injunctions which, if Andromeda observed each of them to the letter, would result in her never riding at all.

Yet her homeland was nothing like this. Joppa was rocky, its vegetation prickly and scarce, its soil overmixed with sand and dried for a thousand years in an unforgiving sun. But this was a lush, green paradise, with gently rolling hills, shady woods, murmuring streams. As she clipped along on a leaf-strewn forest path, she could see why the Hyperboreans had settled here. She could imagine settling here herself, she and—

Andromeda shook her head to dispel the thought. Why did she persist in doing this, linking her name with Perseus? Their fates weren't interwoven. He was so different from her, almost her opposite in many ways.

The path led up to the crest of a ridge that looked out over a valley where the morning mists were still rising. She dismounted and tethered her mare within easy reach of sweet grass, then found a place for herself beneath an oak.

How thrilling the dance had been last night. If Perseus were a different sort of person, more cultured, more sophisticated, she would have enjoyed talking with him about it afterward. But the Muse's Dream had probably meant nothing to him. He'd sat there silently through the whole thing, and when they got back to Eumelus's house, he'd just gone to bed without a word.

Oh, Perseus was good-hearted enough, a simple, honest fellow, but he could never appreciate the finer things. He'd see nothing special in this glorious morning, for instance, nothing special in that hawk up there. It was riding the warm currents of air that rose from the valley below. Barely moving its wings, it soared in a lazy spiral hundreds of feet above the ground. So wondrous, so ethereal, but to Perseus it would just be another bird. Andromeda sighed, leaned back against the massive trunk, and closed her eyes.

Meanwhile, the hawk spotted a hapless sparrow flitting over the branches far below. The sharp-eyed predator folded its wings back and dropped like lightning from a cloudless sky, snaring the smaller bird in mid-flight and killing it instantly with its pointed talons.

Unaware of this small drama, Andromeda stretched, rose to her feet, and scanned the horizon. This looked like the ridge, so she should be able to see it from here, according to Eumelus. A great curiosity he'd called it, and the home of three beautiful goddesses who bless all lovers who visit. Andromeda didn't feel much like a lover, but Eumelus had been so enthusiastic that she wanted to see it.

With her hand she blocked the sun and surveyed the countryside, but could distinguish nothing unusual among the endlessly rolling hills. She untied the mare and gave the landscape one final sweep with her eyes. That's when she spotted it.

Miles away in a broad, upland plain stood something unlike anything she'd ever seen before. It might have been taken for a temple at first, a round, ruined temple, for the roof was gone. Yet it was not really a building at all. Suddenly quite curious, Andromeda remounted and directed her mare's steps toward the strange formation.

* * *

He never anticipated something like this. Hovering in the air a thousand yards from it, Perseus shuddered. He had expected something random—a chaos of bent, twisted rocks, reflecting in their tortured shapes the final gasp of those unfortunate souls who chanced here. He had not foreseen such regularity, such geometry, such hellish symmetry. The outermost ring of boulders, set upright in the earth, supported a continuous circular stone lintel a hundred feet in diameter. Within was a second, incomplete circle, a horseshoe shape, as tall as the outer ring. Who could have imagined that the Gorgons would play architects, translating their victims into faceless, blank monoliths, grotesque building blocks in a monument to their own curse? What bizarre whimsy, born in their anguished souls, had created this diabolic shrine?

Perseus had come upon it unawares. After leaving Eumelus he'd anxiously headed north, but with no idea how far to go or even what he was looking for. Stones? Stones were everywhere. They rested on every hillside, lay tumbled at the bottom of every valley, were strewn along every streambed. But stones did not interest Perseus. What he was really looking for—what, indeed, he would have given anything to see—was a lone woman on a horse. Lulled by the apparent tranquility, the unthinking complacency of the people, he had let Andromeda go off by herself. Now he blamed his own stupidity as he furiously zigzagged over the countryside, scanning the fields, peering through the forest canopy, hoping to catch a glimpse of her. But the land was too broad, the wood too deep. To get a better view, Perseus rose higher in the air, higher than he had ever flown before, and that's when he saw it.

The only comfort was that at least Andromeda was not yet here, and if he worked quickly, he might finish the grim job before she arrived. Perseus twisted the shield around on his arm so that the shiny surface faced him. Holding it out to the side, he located the stone circle on the bronze disk. Then with a deep breath he slowly glided toward it.

Polished though the metal was, and smooth as the armorer's skill could render it, the shield provided at best a distorted view of things. Images were clearest at the center, doubtful near the edge, and apparent distances were deceptive. Perseus tested the mirror by glancing from seen objects on the ground to their image on the disk.

When he was within fifty yards of the circle, Perseus paused, pulled the Cap of Invisibility from his belt and fitted it onto his head. Once more he experienced the queer sensation of not seeing the lower part of his face in his field of vision. He started forward, raised the shield again, then halted abruptly in mid-air. The shield had disappeared.

* * *

The gods, he thought bitterly as he retreated. The great, immortal gods of Olympus, eating ambrosia, drinking nectar, living in joy forever! The great, glorious gods, all-seeing, all-knowing! Yet they hadn't seen, apparently didn't know that this cap they sent him five thousand miles to retrieve would render their other gift, the shield, useless!

He landed at the edge of the woods, lifted the cap from his

head, and immediately the shield reappeared on his arm. He thrust the cap back on. The shield disappeared, along with his sword, his leather bag, his belt, his tunic, his sandals, everything, in fact, that touched him. The gods, in their infinite wisdom, had prescribed two weapons that canceled each other out. All he saw was the tall grass of the plain, waving idly in the wind. Perseus dashed the shield to the ground in disgust, and then threw the cap on top of it.

His plan had been to fly over the stone circle invisibly and locate the Gorgons inside, but now that strategy was abandoned. If he wore the cap, he would not be able to use the shield-mirror, and if he didn't wear the cap, *he* might be the one spotted first, since he would be out in the open for all to see.

The image rose before his eyes again, the wall painting of the Gorgons from Samos, and he felt the cold fear. Perhaps it would be best to leave this hateful plain right now. Surely it would do no harm if he returned to the village for the night. A good sound sleep might clear his head, suggest to him a new, alternate plan that he could put into effect tomorrow. The idea seemed reasonable, tempting. Why not postpone the encounter? Why not go back to carefree Eumelus's house, to that groaning table, that warm bed, that village where there were no swords?

The gray stones loomed in the distance. Perseus knew very well that if he left now, he would never return.

Since a flyover was ruled out, there was only one other way to approach the structure, and that was on foot. Besides, the same stones that hid the monsters could, of a need, provide cover for him. The Gorgons *might* not see him coming. It was a thin strategy, but it was all he had.

Perseus picked up the cap and stuffed it into his belt, then hefted the shield. Slowly he left the shelter of the woods and ventured out onto the plain.

XIX
Medusa

WHAT INSANE LOTTERY was it that decided who was killed, who spared? Eumelus had been here and lived to tell about it. Presumably others too. Did the Gorgons let the laughing groups pass by, only to strike a solitary walker? Did they reserve their wrath for lovers, seeking a perverse revenge for the divine love that had damned them? Or was the deadly selection based on something more commonplace? Did some lucky visitors depart unharmed merely because the monsters were not at home? As Perseus crept toward the stone circle, he realized that they could as easily be watching him from the woods he'd just left.

The closest of the pillars towered twenty feet high. Perseus skulked into its shadow and gingerly brushed it with his fingertips.

Immediately he drew back his hand as if he had been burned. Heated by the sun, the stone was warm like the living creature it had once been.

Suddenly there was a noise on the other side of the boulder. Perseus flattened himself against the rough surface and held his breath. It was a faint but persistent scratching on the ground. He inched his way to the edge of the rock and slowly extended the shield-mirror into the open space. The scratching ceased. Then came a terrific screech as an indistinct black form flew toward him from the polished surface of the bronze. He jerked the shield back and squeezed his eyes shut, as wings beat near his face. Then he heard the familiar call of a crow. Opening his eyes again, he caught sight of it, still complaining as it escaped skyward.

Perseus fell back against the boulder and waited for his heart to stop pounding. He gripped the shield once more, thrust it out into the open, and passed between the stones into the circle.

* * *

It was like a colonnade in a giant's garden. As he wandered in this unnatural grove, Perseus was dwarfed by the massive rocks, any one of which might conceal a creature as large as himself. He panned the shield, searching its polished surface for anything unusual. Carefully, quietly, he picked his way toward the open end of the central horseshoe and slid up to the great silent column that formed the terminus of the right leg. He held the shield at arm's length and pushed it slowly past the rock while peering into its surface. As the interior dimly came into view, he made out the corner of what appeared to be a low rock slab, something like an altar. He twisted the shield slightly to see more of it, but abruptly stopped. Something stirred upon the stone block.

He squinted, frustrated by the distortion in the shield. Perhaps he was mistaken. Maybe it was a just a trick in the mirror, a fault in the bronze. But no, there it was again. The movement seemed oddly familiar, an idle roll, followed by a kind of settling down—the motion of someone asleep. And now he could distinguish a rope-like form dangling from the stone slab nearly to the ground. It appeared to be a braid.

He gasped. Andromeda *is* here, and she's picked *this* of all places to take a nap!

Perseus bounded out from behind the pillar and was just about to shout her name, when he caught sight of something that made him freeze. Of its own accord the braid suddenly rose into the air. Dead still, transfixed, Perseus stared into the shield.

The slumbering figure was not Andromeda, nor were they braids that sprang with such abundance from her scalp, but a profusion of writhing vipers. With scaled wings, curved talons, her tongue protruding hideously even in sleep, Medusa jerked and twitched on the slab, while her two sisters sprawled upon the ground nearby. Perseus had seen the picture of her on Samos, had studied it to the point of revulsion, but the picture, terrifying as it was, glossed over the real horror. It was not so much that Medusa was ugly, for there is much that is ugly in the world. More shocking was the ghastly attractiveness of her, the dreadful femininity.

She was naked, and despite the monstrous alterations—the scales, the scars, the discolored skin—she had the form of a woman. Appalled by his own reaction, Perseus could not tear his eyes away from the image on the disk. Lingering upon her pendulous breasts, her rounded hips and thighs, the dark, hairy cleft between, he was bewitched by a kind of revolting comeliness in her. He wanted a better look.

Perseus advanced into the central clearing. The three sleeping figures took no notice of him, but the snakes, bearing some petty intelligence of their own, began to stir on the Gorgon's heads. They stood on end, bobbed, waved from side to side jockeying with their fellows to get a view of him as he approached. Twelve feet from the stone slab, Perseus stopped, and the serpents, true to their nature, each froze in its latest posture. A hundred pairs of tiny black eyes fastened upon him.

Mesmerized, Perseus wanted to see Medusa more clearly, to look at her directly without the distorting medium of the mirror. Fatal though his gaze might be, it seemed worth the terrible cost. Slowly, dreamily, Perseus lowered the bronze disk to his side. Slowly, dreamily, he turned his eyes toward the stone slab, toward Medusa.

Even as he did so, a sound intruded upon his consciousness. Muffled, indistinct at first, it was coming from outside the stone circle. Perseus tried to focus his attention upon it. The rhythmic sound grew louder. Then, amidst the distracted tangle of his thoughts, he recognized it—hoofbeats.

With a start Perseus jerked his head away and thrust the shield back in place. The Gorgons were still asleep, but the figure upon the slab rolled again, disturbed by the noise. Perseus's mind raced. Andromeda must not come inside, yet he dared not cry out to her. He bolted, dodging the stones like a giant maze, zigzagging to the exterior where he stopped for a moment and listened. The noise had ceased. He dashed around the perimeter of the circle and nearly ran into the horse, standing placidly next to a stone and pulling up the long grass of the plain, but Andromeda was nowhere to be seen.

Perseus tore back inside, nearly colliding with the boulders in his path. At the horseshoe again he paused behind the rightmost pillar. Between the columns on the opposite side, he spotted Andromeda picking her way toward the center, just about to step into the clearing.

"*NOOO!!!* " He leapt into the air and landed directly in front of her, blocking her view with his body.

"Perseus!"

"Hold this!" he shouted, thrusting the shield into her hands, "and don't move! Just hold it in front of your face—like this—and close your eyes tight! Whatever you do, *don't look!* "

Suddenly frightened, Andromeda took the shield and did as he commanded. Then she caught the sound that made her blood run cold, made her want to shut her eyes indeed, and wish herself safely beneath the covers of her bed back in Joppa, or anywhere else than where she stood right now. It was a great, tormented howl of rage, so deep, so ancient, that it might have come from the earth itself.

Perseus leapt back, yanked the cap from his belt and pulled it down on his head. Immediately he disappeared, but the shield—held now in Andromeda's hands—remained clearly visible. Perseus drew his sword and positioned himself so that he could see the writhing monster in the bronze surface.

The two sister Gorgons, their wings beating eagerly, watched from the stone slab as Medusa approached the quaking young woman. Her tongue was extended grotesquely before her, as if tasting the air, and the snakes waved hideously about her crown. It was Medusa's eyes, though, that Perseus fixed upon. Lidless and popping, they glared with deranged fury. Yet behind the monstrous wrath lingered something else, a degraded humanity. As he met her strangely expressive, pathetic eyes in the disk, Perseus found himself pitying the creature. His resolve weakened, his sword shook in his hand. Medusa extended a pointed talon and reached for the shield.

The sword went up, and in one furious downward stroke, Perseus caught the Gorgon at the nape of the neck. A great spray of blood spattered the shield and covered Andromeda's gown. With a sickening thud, Medusa's head fell to the earth, and her body, its talon inches from the shield, collapsed upon the ground.

Behind him Perseus heard the sudden savage cries of Medusa's sisters. Averting his eyes he groped for the head. Still retaining their own animation, the snakes wrapped themselves harmlessly around his wrist. He scraped them off and thrust the dripping head into his leather bag.

"Keep your eyes closed!" Perseus hissed to Andromeda.

Squeezing his own eyes shut, he scooped her up in his arms and vaulted into the air, both of them now invisible. Behind them the Gorgons shrieked in grief over their sister's headless corpse.

Perseus and Andromeda heard the Gorgons' cries long after they had put the stone circle behind them, long after they had passed over the white cliffs, leaving the island for good. Indeed, years later, whenever they lay sleepless in the dark, troubled by loneliness or disappointment or heartache of any kind, they would hear those anguished cries again and again.

XX
Seriphos

DICTYS HOISTED THE BUCKET from deep within the stern and dumped it over the gunwale. "Sixteen," he muttered to himself. Shifting his weight to his right foot, then his left, he rocked from side to side, then lowered the bucket one last time. "Seventeen," he said with finality. When the number reached twenty, he would have to haul the ship up and repair the leaks. It would be a big job. He used to depend on Perseus to help him, but now he'd have to do it alone.

With some difficulty Dictys climbed out onto the warm sand and wiped his brow with his sleeve. It was late summer now, nearly two months since Perseus left. No one really believed that he'd gone to capture the Gorgon's head. The king certainly didn't. Convinced that Perseus was planning some treachery, Polydectes had dispatched several ships in pursuit. The last had returned only a week ago, and Dictys feared the worst.

He pulled the water jug from the boat and took a long draft, then glanced up the hillside toward his stone hut, which seemed so much lonelier now. Dictys' mother had told him that he was homely since the day he was born, and he should just reconcile himself to a single life. He had a large, irregular nose that seemed to grow broader and more peculiar the older he got. Great fleshy bags slung under his eyes. His cheeks were pockmarked, and a wart of uncommon magnitude stood upon his forehead.

But if Dictys didn't have a family of his own, at least he had enjoyed looking after Perseus and Danae these many years. When he'd first brought them to safety here in Seriphos, he'd seen to it that they had shelter and food. He'd presented Danae with a pair of goats and instructed her how to care for them, how to get milk, how to make cheese. When Perseus was old enough, he'd taught the boy to swim, to fish, to sail. But now Perseus was gone and Danae—

"*Dictys!*"

The startled old man saw two figures far up the beach hurrying toward him. He squinted, then the jug of water slipped from his hand.

Perseus ran the last dozen yards and nearly leapt at his old friend. Dictys hesitated at first, as if he'd seen a ghost. But then, tears in his eyes, he wrapped his arms around Perseus. "You're alive," he whispered.

Perseus introduced him to Andromeda, a princess, he said, from Joppa. Yet she wasn't dressed like a princess. Her gown was torn and bloodstained—but with whose blood? They sat in the sand, and Perseus began to relate an extraordinary story about visits from the gods, soaring through the air like a bird, fighting a sea serpent, meeting eyeless hags at the world's end, and finally slaying Medusa in an infernal ring of stones.

Dictys stared at him, trying to comprehend it all. "Then you've really done it."

"Yes, and I've brought the damned head for Polydectes. I hope the bastard's satisfied. But I'd better get home now and let Mother know I'm back." Perseus reached over and patted the old man's knee. "Everything's going to be all right." He stood up.

"Wait." Dictys accepted Andromeda's help as he hauled himself to his feet. "Perseus, your mother's not home."

"Well, where is she?"

"She's at Zeus's temple."

"Then I'll go to the temple."

"You don't understand. The temple's surrounded by soldiers."

"Surrounded? Why?"

"I'm sorry, Perseus. There was nothing I could do." Dictys lowered his eyes, his anguish clear. "The king ordered your mother to the palace. Rather than go, she sought sanctuary in the temple. Polydectes couldn't violate the holy precinct by taking her away by force, but he stationed troops around it. He's waiting to starve her out."

"*Starve her?!* How long has she been there?"

"Nearly a week."

Dictys peered at his old friend's face and was fairly shocked by what he saw. This was no longer boyish vexation. On Perseus's features sat a strangely serene look of menace.

"Do you have any food with you?" Perseus demanded.

"A loaf of bread."

"Get it."

Dictys pulled the loaf out of the boat and handed it to him. "You won't be able to get into the temple. There are too many of them."

Perseus picked up Dictys' water jug and gave it to Andromeda, who then climbed upon his back. "I'll get in."

* * *

The Temple of Zeus was a modest stone structure built halfway up the hill that led to the palace. Soldiers lounged on the temple steps, while others were gathered in knots of two or three around the perimeter of the building. Perseus pulled the cap from his belt and fitted it on his head. Immediately, he and Andromeda vanished. After descending nearly to ground level, they floated easily through the main entrance, inches from the oblivious soldiers.

As their eyes adjusted to the dim light within, they began to make out the single icon that dominated the interior of the temple, a crudely executed wooden statue of Zeus. It depicted a rather unattractive god of stubby proportions whose face, due to a widening crack in the wood, appeared to sport a crooked grin. It stood upon an oversized stone pedestal in the center of the chamber. Also upon that pedestal was the prostrate figure of a woman.

Perseus ran to her. Relieved to find his mother warm and breathing, he cradled her head in his arms while Andromeda lifted the jug of water to her lips. Suddenly alive to the moisture, Danae began to suck at it greedily and had to be restrained from gulping too much at once.

Her thirst satisfied, Danae turned to the smiling young woman holding the jug and eyed her up and down. "Who the hell are you?"

"Mother, it's me," Perseus said, leaning over her. "I'm back."

Danae peered blankly at the inverted face looking down at her. Then for the briefest moment her eyes widened in recognition. Her hand stirred too, as if she were about to reach up to touch the face and satisfy herself that it was real. Instead her glance strayed to the grotesquely grinning statue looming above. Under her breath she murmured, "I owe you one."

"Mother," prodded her son, "don't you recognize me?"

She glimpsed him again. "How am I supposed to recognize you when your face is ass-backwards?" Perseus helped her up to a seated position now and knelt down in front of her. She examined his features. "Come to think of it, I rather prefer you the other way round."

"Are you all right, Mother?"

"Of course I'm all right," she said, dusting off her chiton.

He produced the loaf of bread. "We brought you some food. You must be starved. When was the last time you ate anything?"

"This morning."

"This morning?"

"I've been eating the temple grain." She gestured vaguely toward the shadowed area behind the statue.

"God, Mother, that stuff's been here for ages! It must be full of bugs."

"It's not too bad—if you're very, very hungry. I ran out of water, though, yesterday. Or was it the day before? Time flies when you're having fun." She fixed Perseus with her gaze. "Where have you been, anyway? Dictys told me some cock-and-bull story about the Gorgons. And how did you get in here?"

"Mother, listen, I haven't got time to talk right now. I'm going to leave you for a little while, but I won't be gone long."

Danae regarded him skeptically.

"Do you understand me, Mother?" He repeated the words: "I—won't—be—gone—long. Do you understand what I'm saying?"

"No," she declared. "I went senile while you were away. Hadn't you heard? It happens like that to us old folks. One day we're walking around understanding complicated sentences like 'I won't be gone long,' and the next day we're making nasty puddles on the floor."

Perseus rose and strode toward the entrance.

"Where are you going?" Danae called after him.

"Don't worry about anything. Andromeda's going to take care of you till I get back."

Danae watched as her son disappeared from the temple. Then she turned once more to the young woman holding the water jug. She arched an eyebrow. "*Who's* going to take care of me?"

Calmly the other replied, "Andromeda is."

XXI
Blood Ties

"IT DOESN'T SOUND LIKE PERSEUS." Danae tore a piece of bread from the loaf. "None of what you told me sounds like Perseus. He used to be afraid to kill a spider. I can't imagine him slaying monsters."

"Maybe he's changed."

Danae cast a distrustful eye on her young companion, who was leaning against a pillar watching her. "And you're a princess."

"Yes, of Joppa."

"I think I've heard of Joppa. It's one of those petty kingdoms along the coast of Phoenicia, isn't it?"

"I'm surprised you've heard of it at all," Andromeda replied. "I don't suppose people on Seriphos have much contact with the outside world."

A flash of anger shot through Danae's face, but she squelched it. "Well, it was nice of you to keep my son company in any case. He's had very little experience with girls, as you probably know."

"He did all right."

Danae looked at her. "He did?"

"Yes."

She was silent for several moments, then shrugged her shoulders. "Well, that's a relief. I wondered when it was finally going to happen. The boy's twenty, for God's sake. It's about time he did it with someone—*anyone*."

"Wait a minute. If you think—"

"Oh, don't feel bad about it. There's no need to explain. You were alone, there was moonlight, he whispered a couple of sweet but ungrammatical things in your ear, and before you knew it, you were counting stars in a very undignified posture. I understand how these things happen."

"I'll *bet* you do."

"The less said about it the better," Danae continued. "As soon as we leave this dismal place, we'll see about getting you a passage home, and you can forget all about it."

"I'm not *going* home."

"Why not? Your parents must be worried sick about you."

"My parents want me to marry my uncle."

"So, what's wrong with that? I had an uncle once who was ... quite attractive." Unconsciously Danae smoothed her hair as she said it.

"Well, Phineus isn't. He has no teeth."

"At least he won't bite you."

Andromeda threw her a disgusted glance.

"You'll have to marry someone," the older woman told her. "What will you do? How will you live? There's not much call for unemployed princesses."

"I'll get by."

Danae scrutinized her. "You're not interested in Perseus, are you?"

"Of course not."

"I know it must have been romantic at the time, but you have to remember that it only happened because the two of you were thrown together like that. Under ordinary circumstances you wouldn't have much in common."

"We have *nothing* in common."

"Yes, that's just what I mean. Of course, that's not to say that you can't have fond memories. Everyone recalls their first time, no matter who it's with. Long after Perseus has forgotten your name, he'll probably still remember—"

"Listen," Andromeda snapped, "I'm not interested in your son. I'm a princess, in case you've forgotten, and he's just a ..."

"Just a what, Princess?"

"A peasant," Andromeda concluded. Then she added, "Like you are."

"Like *I* am!" Danae's eyes burned, and she tried to rise from the pedestal, but dizziness from her recent ordeal made her think better on it. She steadied herself with her hands as she sat down shakily and glared at Andromeda. "Hear this, slight offspring of the insignificant potentate of inconsequential Joppa: for your information I'm a daughter of the royal house of Argos."

Andromeda looked doubtful.

"Yes," Danae continued, "and not only that, but I have no siblings, which means that 'peasant' son of mine is not only a prince, but also the heir to the most powerful throne in Greece. Still want to compare pedigrees, Princess?"

"If that's true, why didn't Perseus ever mention it?"

Danae hesitated, then snorted slightly. "Because I don't think he believes it."

"Then why should *I* believe it?"

"Do you know the genealogy of your family, Andromeda?"

"Of course I do."

"All the way back to the gods?"

"Yes, of course."

"Have you ever known a peasant to keep track of such things?"

"No."

Danae took a deep breath. "My father is Acrisius, King of Argos. His father was Abas, King of Argos before him, and his father Lynceus was King of Argos before him. Lynceus married his cousin Hypermnestra, and they were children of the twin brothers Aegyptus and Danaus, Danaus being the first of our line to rule in Argos. These twins were the eldest offspring of Belus, King of Chemmis in the Thebaid, and Belus, rest his shade, was son to the god Poseidon. I could give you more detail, but that's the basic outline. Satisfied, O Miss Highborn?"

Andromeda stared at her, a look of bewilderment on her face. She turned and nervously paced the shadowed interior of the temple, then suddenly halted. "Belus! Did you say Belus?"

"Yes, Belus, son of Poseidon. He married—"

"Oh my God!"

"What is it?"

"Belus married Anchinoe, daughter of Nilus."

"Yes, that's right. How did you know that?"

"Because he's my ancestor too. My father, Cepheus, is descended from Belus. You and I are related." Dazed, she made her way back to the pedestal and sat down. "And that means Perseus and I are related."

"Well, distantly. So what?" Danae asked. "Many royal families are related."

"I'm just thinking about what an old seer told me before I left Joppa."

"Don't believe everything seers tell you. What did he say?"

"That I'd marry a relative and have five sons."

Danae eyed her for several moments. Slowly her face softened, and she slid over next to Andromeda. "Maybe it's time for me to tell you a little more about Perseus's ancestry." She glanced up at the curiously grinning statue above them. "On his *father's* side."

* * *

The royal palace of Seriphos stood at the very top of the hill, overlooking the harbor far below. Two soldiers guarded the gate, and when Perseus asked them if he could see Polydectes, they informed him curtly that the king was unavailable today. He had a distinguished visitor from the mainland and wasn't to be disturbed. When Perseus told them his name, however, they exchanged glances, and one of them was dispatched to the king. The guard returned almost immediately with two more soldiers who escorted Perseus inside.

What passed for a council chamber in the palace was really just the dining hall, with the long wooden tables pushed to one side. Fragments of meat and bread and vegetables, dropped from the tables during meals, were strewn about and ground under people's feet into the dirt floor, which left a lingering smell of rotting garbage in the air.

Perseus remembered this chamber, for it was here on that ill-fated day when Polydectes had demanded the Gorgon's head. Today Perseus had neither the moral support of his fellow citizens, nor the limited safety that their presence provided. Instead the room was filled with the king's retainers, a dozen rogues who eyed him with hostility as he was escorted into the room.

Indistinguishable from this company except for the bronze coronet he wore was Polydectes. Near him stood a white-haired old man, obviously the visiting dignitary, for he had an aristocratic bearing and was attended by his own small but smartly dressed retinue. As Perseus was escorted in, the visitor watched him closely, with an odd blend of curiosity and discomfort.

With a signal from Polydectes, the guards accompanying Perseus stripped him of his sword and shield. Then they stood on either side of him as the King of Seriphos stepped forward.

Polydectes was a short, squat ruffian of fifty with a potbelly and strong, beefy arms. He wore a coarse, not overly clean tunic, which better suited his humble origins than the office he now held. He had acquired the throne by murdering the rightful king twenty years before and had retained his position partly by force, partly by a skillful brand of peasant cunning. Basically a simple man without pretensions or luxurious tastes, Polydectes had used his very commonness to his advantage. Shunning ostentation, he inspired little envy in the populace, and in fact garnered some grudging admiration for his plainness. Also he distributed favors regularly to those citizens who might be most in a position to threaten him, thereby making them party to his tyranny. When he was forced to exert his power, he was circumspect about it, letting its effect fall upon a single victim as an example, and preferably someone low on the social ladder, without friends to avenge him. The young man who stood before him now was just such an individual.

"Where have you been, Perseus?" the king asked. "Rumor had it you were dead."

"I went to the Land of the Hyperboreans."

"What for?"

"To get the Gorgon's head—as you commanded."

Derisive laughter rose from several quarters, but the king did not remove his eyes from Perseus. "And did you get it?"

"Yes. It's here." He patted the leather bag.

"Well, then, hand it over."

Perseus untied the bag from his belt, but hesitated. "Why is my mother imprisoned in the temple?"

"Imprisoned? She's not imprisoned. She can leave anytime she wants to."

"The temple's surrounded by soldiers," Perseus argued. "If she comes out, you'll bring her here."

"That's right."

"Why?"

A sly smile sprouted on Polydectes' face. "Why? Why else but that I want to marry her."

Perseus glared. "She'd rather die than marry you!"

There was a stir around the room, but Polydectes did not alter his expression. Over his shoulder he grinned at the visiting dignitary. "Children! They can never understand a parent's remarriage."

Several of the king's retainers sniggered.

"If I give you Medusa's head," Perseus bargained, "will you call the soldiers off and let my mother go home?"

This was occasion for hoots of laughter around the room. It ceased when the king stepped closer to Perseus, his look menacing. "You take me for a fool, don't you? What have you got in the bag? A monkey's head with a few dead garden snakes sewn on? Is that it? And what did you say to yourself while you were putting the monstrosity together? This will fool the stupid king? Is that what you said, Perseus? The stupid king will never know the difference?" Polydectes leaned still closer now, his foul breath in Perseus's face. "Well, the stupid king isn't so stupid that he can't get between your mother's legs."

Perseus flung down the leather bag and lunged at him, but he was immediately seized by the two guards, who roughly pinioned his arms.

Polydectes calmly returned to the aristocratic visitor and conferred with him quietly, each of them throwing an occasional glance at the struggling captive. The king stepped up to Perseus again.

"It's quite fortunate that you should show up today. Fortunate for us, that is, not for you. This gentleman," he said, indicating the white-haired old man, "came here to offer a very large reward for your head, a reward we thought we would have to forego. But now, thanks to you, we'll be able to collect it."

"My head?"

"Oh, not that one," Polydectes added, following his glance down to the leather bag on the floor. "Your *own* head, Perseus."

"*My* head? But why? What did I do?"

Polydectes hefted the bag and examined it. "I think yours will fit quite nicely in this." He addressed the visitor: "Shall we put it in here for you?"

The old man, who continued to watch Perseus with an apprehensive stare, nodded.

"Ironic, wouldn't you say?" Polydectes continued, grinning at the bag in his hand. "You come here trying to peddle this fraud, when your own head is far more valuable." He untied the cord.

"Wait a minute," Perseus warned him. "Don't open that!"

"Why not? I thought this was for me."

"No! Don't take it out!"

"I'd like to see Medusa's head. We'd *all* like to see it." At that cue the crowd whooped their rowdy approval. Polydectes lifted up the bag and reached into it.

"*Don't!*" Perseus shouted. Breaking free from his captors he made a desperate leap for the leather bag and succeeded in snagging it, but the king had a firm grip on what was inside. As Perseus fell to the floor clutching the bag, the snaky head remained behind, raised high in the air for all to see.

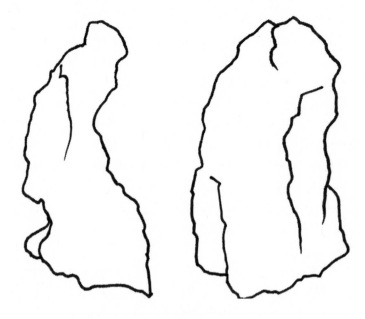

XXII
Orphans

No SOUND, NO MOVEMENT, not even a breath. One moment the chamber had been reverberating with raucous laughter and noise, and the next there was dead quiet.

His eyes squeezed shut and his hands still gripping the crumpled leather, Perseus lay upon the dirt floor, too shocked to move. He wanted to bolt from the room and never look back, but he had to retrieve the Gorgon's head. Slowly he crept toward the spot where the king had been standing. With his hand he groped blindly in front of him until he touched the rough hardness of a stone.

Perseus shrank back in horror. After a moment he overcame his fear and touched it again. Rising to his feet, he ran his hand up the stone until he felt the head suspended near the top. Immediately the snakes wrapped around his wrist. With a tug, he loosed the head from its rocky grip and thrust it back into the leather bag. Then he opened his eyes and was overcome by a wave of nausea.

The chamber, which had been filled so recently with animated, living beings, seemed now the macabre landscape of a nightmare. Boulders, inert and motionless, stood randomly around the room, and in their hideous silence they seemed to mock the single living creature in their midst. Though the stones retained little of their former shapes, yet Perseus thought he could see in them human gestures and attitudes, appalling now in their transformation. The rock closest to him, what had been Polydectes, was a squat but upright stone, and Perseus saw in it the outline of the king's thick torso. Behind it stood what had been the strange old man. It leaned toward him, as if still leveling a queer, anxious stare. He turned away in revulsion.

Hurriedly Perseus tied the leather bag to his belt. Hurriedly he retrieved his sword and shield from where the guards had stashed them. Hurriedly he drew the circular cap from his belt and pulled it upon his head. Then he fled from the chamber.

* * *

Dictys had made it a rule never to sail at night. He'd misjudged the hour once when fishing and nearly foundered upon the rocks in the dark. But tonight he'd broken his rule. They were a mile or so from shore already, Dictys in the stern holding the rudder, Danae at the bow with Perseus and Andromeda.

By means of his cap and his winged sandals, Perseus had smuggled first his mother and then Andromeda out of the temple, and the three had prevailed upon Dictys to take them off the island on his boat. Now they all gazed back toward Seriphos across the widening expanse of black water.

"Where will we go?" Andromeda asked Perseus.

"Melos. Dictys said we could probably settle there."

"What's Melos?"

"Melos," Danae broke in, "is another dirt poor island south of here. With a little luck, we'll land there before morning. With more luck, we'll miss it altogether in the dark."

"Have you got a better idea?" Perseus asked irritably. "I came back here to save you. How was I supposed to know there was a price on my head?"

"How did you come to have a price on your head anyway?"

"I don't know. I'd never even seen the man before, the one who offered the reward. He seemed to know me though, the way he looked at me, and he was in one hell of a hurry to get my head chopped off."

"Maybe he was from Joppa." Danae glanced at Andromeda. "Maybe your parents sent him. What did he look like?"

"He was old."

"Very helpful. What else? Was he tall? Short? Fat? Thin?"

"Tall and thin."

"How was he dressed?"

"He was well dressed. A nobleman, I'd guess."

"What were his clothes like?"

Perseus thought for a moment. "Green."

"Green? No one wears green clothes, even in Joppa."

"No, his clothes weren't green. They were white—"

"Oh, well, anyone could make that mistake."

"But there was an odd green pattern across the bottom."

Danae looked at him, her face suddenly quite serious. "How do you mean, odd?"

"It was braided, sort of. Two green stripes braided together. And every foot or so a leaf in gold."

Danae's brow furrowed. "You said he seemed to recognize you, this old man?"

"Yes, but I'd never laid eyes on him before."

"Describe his face."

"Thin, with kind of sunken cheeks, and a pointy nose—very pointy. And his chin: he had a line down the center of it. I couldn't tell if it was a dimple or an old scar." He turned to Andromeda. "Does he sound like anyone from Joppa?"

Andromeda shook her head.

"I don't see how it matters much anyway," Perseus muttered. "Even if we knew where he was from, we still can't go back home. I'd be blamed for what happened."

Danae had fallen silent, looking out over the water. Wordlessly she rose from the bench and made her way back to Dictys at the stern.

"Perseus," Andromeda said quietly, "your mother told me something today while we were waiting for you in the temple."

"Well, don't believe everything she says. My mother's a notorious liar. What did she tell you?"

"She told me about your ancestry."

"You mean the famous Royal House of Argos?"

"She told me that, but she also told me about the Shower of Gold. Is it true?"

"I don't know. Hermes said it was true, but Hermes is a bigger liar than my mother is. What's the difference? Even if Almighty Zeus is my father, it's not going to raise my status any, if that's what you're thinking."

"I don't care about your status."

He looked at her doubtfully. Then in silence they watched the prow of the boat as it parted the dark waves before them. Andromeda shivered. Perseus reached behind for the blanket and draped it around her. She raised an edge toward him. "Come on, there's room."

He slid next to her. After a while he glanced over his shoulder at Danae, who was now stretched out on a long bench amidships and dozing.

"So, what did you think of my mother?"

"I can get used to her."

"She has that effect on everybody." He lowered his voice. "Listen, Andromeda, I've been thinking. Where we're going—it'll be hard for someone on her own. I mean, especially someone who's not used to it."

"I'll manage."

"Well, what I wanted to say was—"

He broke off suddenly, squinting at the stars overhead.

"What's the matter?" Andromeda asked.

"We've changed course."

"Are you sure?"

"Of course I'm sure. We're not heading south anymore. We're heading ... west." Perseus turned around. "Dictys," he hissed, trying not to wake his mother, "did we change course?"

The old man nodded.

"Why?"

Pointing with his chin, Dictys indicated the recumbent figure on the bench.

"My mother told you to change course? Where are we going?"

Dictys mouthed a word, but Perseus could not hear it over the sound of the waves. He cupped his hand behind his ear and repeated, "*Where?*"

The old man formed the word on his lips again, but still Perseus could not make it out. "I can't hear you," he whispered. "What did you say?"

From amidships came a sleepy voice. "He said Argos."

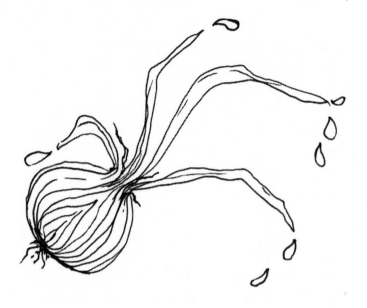

XXIII
Argos

"I SAW A SAIL!" the old lady announced excitedly as she rushed into the kitchen, her cloak swirling about her. "I saw it from the roof."

Two women slicing onions at the table exchanged glances. One of them laid down her knife. "Now you know your ladyship shouldn't be going up on the roof. Didn't his majesty tell you that? You could fall."

"But I saw a sail in the harbor," she insisted.

"That wasn't his majesty's ship. We'll tell you when he returns." The cook got up and guided the queen to a chair. "Why doesn't your ladyship sit down here with us for a while, and I'll get you some nice milk."

From a pitcher on the sideboard she filled an ornate pottery cup and set it before her. The queen fingered it, detected the odor of onions on the rim, and pushed it aside. "Isn't there any wine?"

"You know his majesty doesn't like you drinking wine. He says it's bad for your nerves, and he told me before he left that under no circumstances—"

At that moment a teen-age boy burst into the room. "Some strangers are at the gate!" He noticed the queen. "Oh, I beg your pardon, your ladyship. I didn't know you were here."

"The guards know the king's away," the cook responded.

"But they don't want to see the king. They want to see the mistress."

"That's ridiculous. No one ever—"

The queen stood up. "They want to see *me*?"

"No, no, your ladyship," the cook soothed. "There's got to be a mistake."

"It's no mistake," the boy continued. "The one who did all the talking—and she acted like she owned the place—asked for the mistress by name, Queen Aganippe."

"That's me!" the queen declared.

"Yes, of course, your ladyship, but still there must be some mistake." The cook gave the boy a stern look. "Tell them to leave. They can come back when the king returns."

"*No!* " Aganippe's tone was imperious. "If they're here to see me, I will see them."

"But your ladyship—"

She swept out of the kitchen, then with determined step strode up the broad stone path that led through the courtyard to the principal gate. At her command the startled guards pulled open the great oak double doors. Waiting on the other side was a scruffy party of four: a young man with a bulging pouch dangling from his belt, a young woman in a badly stained gown, a homely old man who smelled of fish, and—

For several moments Aganippe stared at the fourth member of this strange company. Then she whispered, "Oh my God. Danae!"

* * *

"They think I'm crazy," Aganippe laughed as she shut the last of the servants out of the kitchen. "They think I've taken in four complete strangers, given them food, new clothes, and sent three of them off on a grand tour of the palace. They probably can't wait until Acrisius gets back to set things right again." She paused. "I hope you don't mind if we talk in here. It'll be a little more private than that big hall upstairs."

"I don't mind," Danae assured her.

With her fingertips, Aganippe removed the cup of milk from the table and deposited it on the sideboard, sneering at it the while. Then she retrieved a stone jar from the very back of a low shelf. "They hide the wine on me, but since they keep it very convenient for themselves, it's never hard to find." She poured the dark liquid into two fresh cups, then sat with Danae at the table.

"I probably am," she continued. "Crazy, I mean. It's been helpful to be a little crazy, especially with your father. He's been difficult all these years. Now that he thinks I've completely lost my wits, he pays me little heed, but I get very attentive service from the staff." She took a sip of the wine, then put down the cup and gazed lovingly at her daughter. "I've prayed to the gods for this day, Danae, when I'd see you again and see my grandson, but I never thought it would really come."

"I prayed for it too."

"What a fine young man he is! And good looking too, and intelligent."

"Well, don't go overboard."

"I always wondered how he turned out. Remember what a crybaby he was and how scared we were that your father would hear him?"

"I remember."

"Now just look at him! All grown up—and courting already. What's the young lady's name again?"

"Andromeda."

"That's right. Such a lovely girl. But she's much too skinny! You should get her to put on some weight, Danae. Why, the girl has hardly any—you know." Aganippe lifted her cupped hands and held them out before her bosom.

Danae smiled.

"Well, a man likes to see a little ... significance up there. You should really tell her to eat more."

"I'll try, Mother."

"She is pretty, though. And well-connected, you said?"

"A princess."

"Ah, a princess!"

"Of Joppa."

"Oh." A momentary look of disappointment passed over her features. "Well, at least she's a princess. That's what counts. Do you think Perseus will marry her?"

"He'd better. She's already counting her children."

"They'll make a nice couple." Aganippe's face took on a more doubtful cast. "Now, the *older* gentleman," she intoned carefully. "I've wanted to ask you: is he *your* husband?"

"Heavens no, Mother! That's Dictys. Don't you recognize him? He's the fisherman who took Perseus and me away twenty years ago."

Aganippe let out a sigh. "Well, that's good. I'm sure he's a very nice person, but he's so ... unattractive. Not that I hold someone's looks against them, you understand. I mean, no one chooses their looks. What's important is what's on the inside. And if you decided to marry this Dictys for some other—less apparent—qualities that he has, I certainly would never say anything."

"I'm *not* going to marry Dictys, Mother."

Aganippe looked relieved. She took another sip of wine as a look of sadness and resignation overspread her features. "I wish I could ask you to stay, Danae, but I don't dare. I only thank Zeus you came when you did, while your father's away. If you'd come while he was here, I don't like to think of what he would have done—to Perseus."

"What would he have done?"

"He's still worried sick about that hateful prophecy. Oh, how I've cursed the oracle who made it. It's ruined our lives. Ever since he heard it, Acrisius has been a changed man. First building that horrid prison for you, then, after you escaped, terrified that your son would show up here someday and kill him. It's been a nightmare. I think if he got hold of Perseus—"

"What would he do?"

"I think he'd imprison the boy, just as he imprisoned you."

Her daughter was silent.

"I'm serious, Danae. The man is obsessed. If I were you, I'd take my son as far away as you can."

"Where did Father go?"

The queen hesitated. "I'm not supposed to know."

"But you do know."

Aganippe sighed. "Seriphos. That's where you were living, wasn't it?"

Danae lowered her eyes.

"Well, I couldn't be sure," Aganippe continued. "A merchant passing through Argos told your father, and before the merchant left I got the fellow to tell me too, but you know how merchants are. He could have been mistaken, or lying, or anything. Apparently Acrisius had told this man your name and had asked him to inquire for you in his travels. The merchant must have heard about you when he stopped at Seriphos. In any case he told your father that you had a grown son, and that sent Acrisius into a panic. He told everyone that he had to go on an important diplomatic mission to Larissa, but of course I knew better." She paused. "Once he finds out you're not there, he'll return home. You can spend the night, Danae, but for your own safety, I think it would be best for all of you to leave tomorrow."

Danae looked at her mother. "He won't be coming back."

"What?"

"I'm sorry," Danae said quietly. "He's dead. Father is dead."

Aganippe stared at her.

"He didn't go to Seriphos to take Perseus prisoner. He went there to take his life, but by accident Perseus killed him instead."

The queen looked down at the cup of wine quivering in her hands. She sat in silence for some time. Finally she whispered, as much to herself as to her daughter, "The prophecy came true after all." She wiped the single tear that had rolled down her cheek. "You must hate him."

"He tried to kill my son, who never did him any harm."

"Yes. That's unforgivable, I know, and now he's paid for it. He wasn't all bad though, Danae. I want you to know that about him at least. I knew Acrisius better than you did. He was a good king, good to his people, fair, not cruel. He wasn't all bad. I think if he had never heard that damned prophesy—well, who's to say? But it poisoned his mind." She shook her head. "Imagine, trying to kill his own grandson! I'm so sorry, Danae. I apologize to you, for his sake."

Her daughter reached over and took her mother's hand.

"Oh, I'm all right," Aganippe said wearily, wiping her eyes. "In a way I'm relieved. This has been coming for twenty years. Not a day went by that he didn't expect Perseus to show up suddenly. At least it's finally over. His fears are at an end now. He can rest in peace." She patted her daughter's arm. "Life is certainly peculiar, isn't it? When Acrisius and I were first married, all he wanted was for me to bear a son, someone to reign after him. Then he spent the rest of his life fearing that *you* would do just that: bear a son—who, as it turns out, *will* reign after him." A faint, ironic smile formed on her lips. "Perseus is king now. Does he know that?"

Danae shook her head. "He doesn't even know who it was that he killed on Seriphos. From his description I was pretty certain it was Father, especially since he had the royal pattern on his hem, but I had to talk to you first to make sure."

"Well, I'm certain your boy will make a good king, Danae."

"I hope so. I told him we were just visiting here before we settled on Melos. I'm afraid this is going to come as a shock."

* * *

"*King?!*"

"Close your mouth, Perseus," Danae said. "You look like an imbecile. And though being an imbecile is the first prerequisite of kingship, you're not supposed to be quite so blatant about it."

They stood in the courtyard with Andromeda and Dictys, all newly scrubbed and freshly attired.

"I don't want to be king," Perseus protested. "I resign."

"You can't resign. Your grandmother's already told all the servants."

"But I don't know anything about governing."

"Good. That's the second prerequisite."

"I don't understand any of this. What happened to Acrisius, anyway? How did he die all of a sudden?"

"In a freak accident. I'll tell you about it sometime."

Exasperated, Perseus looked to Dictys, then to Andromeda. "*You* probably *want* me to be king."

"No," Andromeda replied calmly.

"You just don't understand," he continued as if he hadn't heard her. "You've been a princess all your life. You grew up expecting to live in a palace, to tell people what to do and sound convincing about it. I spent my life scaling fish and milking goats, and I wasn't even very good at that. Dictys can tell you. Dictys, tell her how bad I was at scaling fish."

"He was very bad at it, Miss."

"There, see what I mean!"

"Perseus, don't be ridiculous," his mother chided. "No one is going to expect you to scale fish as king."

"But I don't want to *be* king!"

"Then why are we waiting around here?" Andromeda asked. "Let's go to Melos like we'd planned."

Perseus looked at her, doubtful. "Do you mean that?"

"Try me."

He shook his head in consternation. "I need to be alone for a while." Perseus strode toward the palace gate, hesitated when the guards bowed low to him. Then, remembering something, he retrieved his sword and shield.

"Expecting trouble?" his mother asked.

"There's still a price on my head, you know."

"Oh," Danae said as she watched her son disappear from the courtyard, "I forgot."

XXIV
Beachcombers

IT WAS PREPOSTEROUS! To be master of that place, to be master
of all Argos, the greatest kingdom in Greece—the whole idea was
absurd. Even the servants intimidated him.

Stalking along an isolated stretch of shoreline, Perseus cast an
eye over his shoulder at the palace. Maybe they *could* just go to
Melos like they'd planned. Why not? On Melos he wouldn't have to
worry about any of this. He could just—

"Hey, Sport, this is where we came in, right?"

Perseus halted, barely surprised by the intruder who had
suddenly appeared by his side.

"You remember," Hermes prodded. "The first day I met you,
you were hoofing along the beach by your lonesome just like this."

"Hello."

"Hello? Gotten kind of blasé, haven't we, about encountering
divinities on our strolls?"

"I figured I'd see you sooner or later."

"Well, it would have been a hell of a lot sooner rather than later if Athena had had her way. That old killjoy wanted me to collect your gear as soon as you'd done in Medusa. Can you believe that? But hell, a deal is a deal, so I waited till you paid your debt to Polydectes. Besides, I wouldn't have missed that for the world—the way you petrified that whole crew of plug-uglies."

"It was an accident."

Hermes waved his hand dismissively. "Don't worry about it. The place is going to smell a whole lot better without them, and it'll be a boon to the Seriphian economy. Long after that shack of a palace has fallen down, the ring of boulders will still be there, and they'll charge tourists big bucks just to see it."

Perseus looked solemn. "You didn't tell me I'd end up a king."

"What would life be without a few surprises? You worried? Listen, don't sweat it. The hardest part about being a king is having to hold in your pee for long periods of time. State functions, you understand."

"Do I have to be king?"

"Nope. You've got free will. None of your predestination in this religion. You pays your money, you takes your choice."

Perseus glanced again at the palace looming in the distance. "If I agree to it, will I be a good king?"

"Beats me. Your chroniclers are completely silent on that score, which probably means that your reign will be neither very good nor very bad. In short, nothing to write home about. I can tell you one thing about the future, though. You're going to be the great-grandfather of Hercules. Yeah, I know what you're thinking: big hot-shit deal, right? So who's this Hercules when he's at home?"

"Who *is* he?"

"A big lummox, really, with the intelligence of a turnip. Makes you look like a Rhodes scholar. He'll get on the wrong side of Hera and have to perform twelve famous labors. No one will ever quite agree on what the twelve famous labors were, but everyone will concur that they were famous and that there were twelve of them. Also in the process he'll go mad and kill his wife and children. This bit of domestic mayhem, by the by, will be dramatized successfully on both the Greek and the Roman stage. Finally, he'll make the fatal mistake of cheating on his second wife, who'll get her revenge by incinerating him in a poisoned mackinaw. For all that, he's going to be the most famous of all Greek heroes. You explain it."

"And he's my great-grandson?"

"Yes. Also your half-brother, if you take my meaning. But time's a-wastin', Sport. I'll relieve you of your impedimenta now, if you don't mind."

Perseus loosened the leather bag from his belt and handed it over.

"Athena will be pleased to get this," Hermes commented, weighing its contents. "She plans to have it embossed right on the center of your shield there so she can tote the damn thing around. Gross, huh? There's no explaining some people. It takes all kinds, I guess."

Perseus slipped the shield from his back, pulled the odd, circular cap from his belt, but when he reached for his sword, Hermes stayed his hand.

"That's yours, Sport. Gift—from me to you."

Perseus shoved the sword back into his belt. When he looked down at the winged sandals, he hesitated. "Do you think I could keep these ... just for a little while longer?"

"Hell, no! The adventure's over. You don't need them anymore. Besides, I thought I might wear them myself. Improve my image, you know? 'Winged Mercury' and all that. Style is everything, after all. What do you want them for anyway?"

He made no answer.

Hermes snorted. "Oh, all right. Keep them until tonight. You can leave them outside your door when you go to bed, and I'll be around to collect them. But no shoe-shine cracks, okay?"

With that, Hermes slung the shield onto his back and stuffed the cap into his belt. "Well, I'd better get these things to her nibs before she throws a fit."

"This is the last time I'm going to see you."

"That's right, Sport. Hey, you're not going to get sentimental on me, are you?" Hermes reached over and touched his shoulder, sending the familiar tingling sensation throughout his body. "You did real good, you know. Especially with Medusa. I was proud of you. I'm the Slayer of Argus, as I'm sure I've mentioned, but the difference between your feat and mine is that Argus couldn't have slain me back. And if you can't die, Sport, then you're not really alive, are you?"

Perseus stared at him.

Hermes gave his shoulder a light squeeze, then dropped his hand. "Gotta blast. You'll find your princess a little ways up the beach."

He hesitated.

"Go ahead," Hermes coaxed. "You're the only man in history who can *literally* sweep a girl off her feet, and this is your last chance. Go for it."

Perseus turned to leave, then looked back at his companion. "Thank you ... for everything."

Hermes grinned. "Don't mention it, Sport."

* * *

As the western sky took on a deepening red, the last rays of the sun lit the tops of the palace walls a burnished gold. From his lofty perspective Perseus could scan nearly the whole of Argos. Ships rocked idly in the harbor, their sails furled, their oars pulled in for the night. On the hillsides were groves of olive trees, vineyards, stone huts, and lines of low rock walls. Flocks of sheep were bedding down in the pasture, while shepherds lit their evening fires. Along the rutted roads farmers trudged home with hearty appetites, the day's work done. And far below on the beach Perseus spotted a lone woman walking slowly along the shore, her lithe silhouette casting a long shadow on the sand.

In an effortless dive Perseus swooped down nearly to ground level. Then like a mild breeze he overtook her from behind, slipped his arms around her waist, and gently as a whisper lifted her into the air.

"Oh my God," she gasped. When she realized what had happened, Andromeda caught her breath and looked around at him. "Perseus, what are you doing? You scared me."

"I want to ask you something."

"Couldn't you ask me on the ground?"

"I'm going to be spending enough time on the ground soon enough."

"So, what do you want to ask me?"

"Did you mean what you said before, about going to Melos?"

"Yes."

"You'd go there with me if I decided not to be king?"

"Yes."

"It's hard for me to believe that you'd really *want* to go there."

"No one said anything about *wanting* to go, Perseus. I'd have to be crazy to prefer that life to this. Even your friend Dictys, who you think is the image of bucolic contentment—even Dictys is hoping you'll stay here so he can hang up his ratty old nets for good and have some leisure in his old age. I don't *want* to go to Melos."

"Then why would you go?"

"You know, Perseus, you can really be dense sometimes. I'd go there with you because I love you."

Stars began to twinkle in the evening sky, their reflections dancing upon the waves below. After a while Perseus banked over the ocean in a broad arc and began heading in the opposite direction.

"Where are we going?" Andromeda asked.

"Back to the palace."

"Why?"

"It's my home now, isn't it?"

"Is it?"

"Yours too," he added, "if you want it."

She twisted around. "Is that a proposal?"

"Yes, it is."

Andromeda smiled, then relaxed in his arms as they both gazed at the coastline passing beneath them. "It'll be strange," she said quietly, "sleeping in a bed every night. I've gotten so used to sleeping in the sand, under the stars."

"We could still do it sometimes if we want to."

"I suppose so, but we probably never will."

The palace loomed in the distance, but Perseus slowed his progress to a stop, hovering for a while in the mild summer air. He and Andromeda looked at each other, then at the expanse of shore below, then at each other again.

Gracefully, unhurriedly, Perseus glided down to the beach.

Richard Matturro, a native of Rye, New York, holds a doctorate in English with a specialization in Shakespeare and Greek Mythology. After sixteen years at the *Albany Times Union*, he now teaches in the English Department at UAlbany and lives on an old farm in the foothills of the Berkshires. *Perseus* is his fourth novel.

Mary Trevor Thomas, a South Dakota native, is a graduate of Smith College and the School of the Museum of Fine Arts in Boston. Her work has been shown in Boston and Munich. She is currently a librarian in the Albany area.